D0259097

MR. GALLIANO'S
CIRCUS

MR. GALLIANO'S
CIRCUS

by
Enid Blyton

PRINTED IN
DEAN & SON Ltd.
41/43 Ludgate Hill LONDON EC4
GREAT BRITAIN
TRADE MARK

TR 600/48

603 03288 5

MADE AND PRINTED IN GREAT BRITAIN BY
PURNELL AND SONS LTD., PAULTON (SOMERSET) AND LONDON

CONTENTS

CHAPTER PAGE

I. THE CIRCUS COMES TO TOWN . . . 7

II. JIMMY MAKES FRIENDS WITH THE CIRCUS FOLK 13

III. JIMMY LEARNS ABOUT CIRCUS WAYS . . . 19

IV. JIMMY SEES THE CIRCUS! 25

V. A SHOCK FOR MR. GALLIANO . . . 31

VI. AN EXCITING NIGHT 38

VII. JIMMY HUNTS FOR JUMBO 45

VIII. JIMMY JOINS THE CIRCUS 51

IX. THE CIRCUS GOES ON THE ROAD . . . 58

X. THE FIRST NIGHT IN THE CARAVAN . . 64

XI. LOTTA GIVES JIMMY A RIDING LESSON . 72

XII. A GOOD TIME FOR THE CIRCUS . . . 79

XIII. POOR OLD PUNCH 86

XIV. THE STRANGE MEDICINE 93

XV. MR. WALLY'S WONDERFUL CHIMPANZEE . 100

XVI. JIMMY GETS A DOG OF HIS OWN . . . 107

XVII. LUCKY GOES TO SCHOOL 115

XVIII. MR. WALLY HAS AN ACCIDENT . . . 122

XIX. WHAT HAPPENED TO SAMMY THE CHIMPANZEE 128

XX. JIMMY GOES INTO THE RING 135

XXI. GOOD OLD LUCKY 142

XXII. LUCKY HAS A CHANCE 149

XXIII. THE WONDERFUL CARAVAN—AND
JUMBO'S SURPRISE 156

XXIV. THE TWO MARVELLOUS BROTHERS . . 164

XXV. LOTTA IS UNHAPPY 171

XXVI. JIMMY AND LOTTA GET THEIR REWARD . . 178

THE CIRCUS COMES TO TOWN

One morning, just as Jimmy Brown was putting away his books at the end of school, he heard a shout from outside:

"Here comes the circus!"

All the children looked up from their desks in excitement. They knew that a circus was coming to their town and they hoped that the circus procession of caravans, cages, and horses would go through the streets when they were out of school.

"Come on!" yelled Jimmy. "I can hear the horses' hoofs! Good-bye, Miss White!"

All the children yelled good-morning to their teacher and scampered out to see the circus procession. They were just in time. First of all came a very fine row of black horses, and on the front one rode a man dressed all in red, blowing a horn. He did look grand!

Then came a carriage that looked as if it were made of gold, and in it sat a handsome man, rather fat, and a plump woman dressed all in pink satin.

"That's the man who owns the circus!" said somebody. "That's Mr. Galliano—and that's his wife! My, don't they look fine!"

Mr. Galliano kept taking off his hat and bowing to all the people and the children round about. Really, he acted just like a king. He had a very fine moustache with sharp-pointed ends that turned upwards. His top-hat was shiny and black. Jimmy thought he was simply grand.

Then came some white horses, and on the first one, leading the rest, was a pretty little girl in a white, shiny frock. She had dark-brown curls, and eyes as blue as the cornflowers in the cottage gardens near by. She made a face at Jimmy, and tried to flick him with her little whip. She hit his wrist.

"You're a naughty girl!" shouted Jimmy. But the little girl only laughed and made another face. Jimmy forgot about her when he saw the next bit of the procession. This was a clown, dressed in red and black, with a high, pointed hat; and he didn't walk along the road—no, he got along by turning himself over and over on his hands and feet, first on his hands and then on his feet, and then on his hands again.

"That's called turning cart-wheels," said Tommy, who was standing next to Jimmy. "Isn't he clever at it? See, there he goes, like a cart-wheel, over and over and round and round!"

Suddenly the clown jumped upright and took off his hat. He turned over on to his hands again, and popped his hat on his feet, which were now up in the air. Then the clown walked quickly along on his hands so that his feet looked like his head with a hat on. All the children laughed and laughed.

Next came a long string of gaily-coloured caravans. How Jimmy loved these! There was a red one with neat little windows at which curtains blew in the wind. There was a blue one and a green one. They all had small chimneys, and the smoke came out of them and streamed away backwards.

"Oh, I wish I lived in a caravan!" said Jimmy longingly. "How lovely it must be to live in a house that has wheels and can go away down the lanes and stand still in fields at night!"

The horses that drew the caravans were not so fine-looking as the black and white ones that had gone in front. Jimmy hardly had time to look at them before there came a tremendous shout down the street:

"There's an elephant!"

And, dear me, so there was! He came along grandly, pulling three cages behind him. He didn't feel the weight at all, for he was as strong as twenty horses. He was a great big creature, with a long swinging trunk, and as he reached Jimmy he put out his trunk to the little boy as if he wanted to shake hands with him! Jimmy was pleased. He wished he had a bun to give the elephant.

The big animal lumbered on, dragging behind it the cages. Two of them were closed cages and nothing could be seen of the animals inside. But one was open at one side and Jimmy could see three monkeys there. They sat

in a row on a perch, all dressed in warm red coats, and they looked round at the children and grown-ups watching them, with bright eyes.

"Look! There's another monkey—on that man's shoulder!" said Tommy. Jimmy looked to where he pointed and, sure enough, riding on the step of the monkey's cage was a funny little man, with a face almost as wrinkled as the monkey's on his shoulder. The monkey he carried cuddled closely to the man and hugged him with its tiny arms. As they passed the children the monkey took off the man's cap and waved it!

"Did you see that?" shouted Jimmy in delight. "That monkey took off the man's cap and waved it at us! Look! It's putting it back on his head now. Isn't it a dear little thing?"

At last the procession ended, and all the horses, cages, and caravans trundled into Farmer Giles's field where the circus was to be held. The children went home to dinner, full of all they had seen, longing to go and see the circus when it opened on Wednesday.

Jimmy told his mother all about it, and his father too. Jimmy's father was a carpenter, and he had been out of work for nearly a year. He was very unhappy about it, for he was a good workman, and he did not like to see Jimmy's mother going out scrubbing and washing to earn money.

"My!" said Jimmy, finishing up his dinner, and wishing there was some more, "how *I'd* like to go to that circus."

"Well, you can't, Jimmy," said his mother. "So don't think any more about it."

"Oh, I know that, Mum," said Jimmy cheerfully. "Don't you worry. I'll go and see the animals and the clown and everything in the field, even if I can't go to the circus."

So after school each day Jimmy slipped under the rope that went all round the ring of circus vans and cages, and wandered in and out by himself. At first he had been shouted at, and once Mr. Galliano himself had come along with his pointed moustache bristling in anger, and told Jimmy to go away.

Jimmy was afraid then, and was just going when he heard a voice calling him from a caravan near by. He turned to see who it was, and saw the curly-haired little girl there.

"Hallo, boy!" she said. "I saw you watching our procession yesterday. Are you coming to the show tomorrow night!"

"No," said Jimmy. "I've got no money. I say—can I just peep inside that caravan! It does look so nice!"

"Come up the ladder and have a peep if you want to," she said. Jimmy went up the little ladder at the back of the caravan and peeped inside. There was a bed at the back, against the wooden wall of the caravan. There was a black stove, on which a kettle was boiling away. There was a tiny table, a stool, and a chair. There were shelves all round holding all sorts of things, and there was a gay carpet on the floor.

"It looks *lovely*!" said Jimmy. "I wonder why people live in houses when they can buy caravans instead."

"Can't think!" said the little girl. Jimmy stared at her—and she made a dreadful face at him.

"You're rude," said Jimmy. "One day the wind will change and your face will get stuck like that."

"I suppose that's how you got your own face," said the little girl, with a giggle. "I wondered how it could be so queer."

"It isn't queer," said Jimmy. "And look here—just you tell me why you hit me with your whip yesterday? You hurt me."

"I didn't mean to," said the little girl. "What's your name?"

"Jimmy," said Jimmy.

"Mine's Lotta," said the girl. "And my father is called Laddo, and my mother is called Lal. They ride the horses in the circus and jump from one to another. I ride them too."

"Oh," said Jimmy, thinking Lotta was really very clever, "I do wish I could come and see you."

"You come this time tomorrow and I'll take you round the circus camp and show you everything," said Lotta. "I must go now. I've got to cook the sausages for supper. Lal will be angry if she comes back and they're not cooked."

"Do you call your mother Lal?" said Jimmy, surprised.

"'Course I do," said Lotta, smiling. "And I call my father Laddo. Everybody does. Good-bye till tomorrow."

Jimmy ran home. He felt most excited. To think that the next day he would be taken all round the circus camp and would see everything closely! That was better than going to the circus.

JIMMY MAKES FRIENDS WITH
THE CIRCUS FOLK

The next day, as soon as afternoon school was over, Jimmy ran off to the circus field. A great tent had been put up. This was where the circus was to be held that night. The circus folk had been very busy all day long, getting everything ready.

Jimmy looked for Lotta. The little man who owned the monkeys came along and he glared at Jimmy.

"You go home just as quickly as ever you can," he said. "Go along! No boys allowed here!"

"But . . . " began Jimmy.

"What! You dare to disobey me, the great Lilliput!" said the little man, and he ran at Jimmy. Jimmy didn't know quite what was going to happen next, but a voice called out from the caravan near by:

"Lilliput! Lilliput! That's my friend! Leave him alone!"

The little man turned round and bowed. "Your pardon," he said. "Any friend of yours is welcome here, dear Lotta."

"Don't be silly, Lilliput!" said Lotta, and the little girl jumped down from the caravan and ran over to Jimmy. "This is Jimmy. And this is Lilliput, Jimmy. He has the monkeys. Where's Jemima, Lilliput?"

"Somewhere about," said Lilliput. "Jemima love! Jemima love! Come along!"

A small, bright-eyed monkey came running out on all-fours from under a cart. She tore over to Lilliput, leapt up to his shoulder and put her arms round his neck.

"This is Jemima," said Lotta. "She is the darlingest monkey in the world—isn't she, Lilliput? And the cleverest."

"That's right," said Lilliput. "I bought her from a black

13

man when I was in foreign lands, and she's just as cunning as can be. Look, Jemima—here's Nobby! Go ride him, go ride him!"

The monkey made a little chattering noise, slipped down to the ground and ran quietly over to a large brown dog who was nosing about the field. She jumped on to his back, held on to his collar and jumped up and down to make him go. Jimmy laughed and laughed.

"Come along!" said Lotta, slipping her bare brown arm through his. "Come and see the clown."

The clown lived in a rather dirty little caravan all by himself. He sat at the door of it, polishing some black shoes he meant to wear that night. He didn't look a bit like a clown now. He had no paint on his face, and he wore a dirty old hat. But he was very funny.

"Hallo, hallo, hallo!" he said, when he saw Jimmy coming. "The Prince of Goodness Knows Where, as sure as I'm eating my breakfast!" He got up and bowed politely.

"But you're not eating your breakfast!" Jimmy laughed.

"Then you can't be the Prince," said the clown. "That just proves it—you can't be the Prince."

"Well, I'm not," said Jimmy. "I'm Jimmy Brown. What's *your* name?"

"I am Sticky Stanley, the world-famous clown," said the clown proudly, and he gave his shoes an extra rub.

"What a funny name!" said Jimmy. "Why do you call yourself Sticky?"

"Because I stick to my job and my friends stick to me!" said Stanley. And he leapt down from his caravan, began to carol a loud song and juggle with his two shoes, his brush, and his tin of polish. He sent them all up into the air one by one and caught them very cleverly, sending them up into the air again, higher and higher.

Jimmy watched him, his eyes nearly falling out of his head. However could anyone be so clever? The clown caught them all neatly in one hand, bowed to Jimmy, and turned two or three somersaults, landing with a thud right inside his caravan.

"Isn't he funny?" said Lotta. "He's always like that. Come and see the elephant. He's a darling."

The elephant was in a tall tent by himself, eating hay contentedly. His leg was made fast to a strong post.

"But he doesn't really need to be tied up at all," said Lotta. "He would never wander away. Would you Jumbo?"

"Hrrrumph!" said Jumbo, and he lifted up his trunk and took hold of one of Lotta's curls.

"Naughty Jumbo!" said Lotta, and she pushed his trunk down again. "Look, this is Jimmy. Say Jimmy, Jumbo."

"Hrrrumph!" said Jumbo, and he said it so loudly that Jimmy's cap flew off in the draught! Jumbo put down his trunk, picked up Jimmy's cap and put it back on his head. Jimmy was so surprised.

"Hrrrumph!" said Jumbo again, and pulled out some more hay to eat.

"He's very clever," said Lotta. "He can play cricket just as well as you can. He holds a bat with his trunk, and hits the ball with it when his keeper, Mr. Tonks, bowls to him. Now come and see the dogs."

Jimmy had heard the dogs long before he saw them. There were ten of them—all terriers. They were in a very big cage, running about and barking. They looked clean and silky and happy. They crowded up to Jimmy when he put his hand out to them.

"That's Darky and that's Nigger and that's Boy and that's Judy and that's Punch and that's . . ." began Lotta. But Jimmy couldn't see which dog was which. He just stood there and let them all lick his hands as fast as they could.

"I take them all out once a day," said Lotta. "They go out five at a time. I have one big lead and they each have a short lead off it, so I can keep them all together. They do pull though!"

"What do they do in the circus!" asked Jimmy.

"Oh, all kinds of things," said Lotta. "They can all walk on their hind legs, and some of them can dance round and round in time to the music. This one, Judy, can jump through hoops held as high as my head. She is very clever."

"I like Judy," said Jimmy, letting the little sandy-headed terrier lick his fingers. "How do they teach the dogs their tricks, Lotta? Do they punish them if they don't do them properly?"

Lotta looked at Jimmy in horror. "Punish them!" she said. "That shows how little you know about a real good circus, Jimmy. Why, we all know that no animals will play or work properly for us unless we love them and are kind to them. If Mr. Galliano saw anyone hitting a dog or a monkey he would send him off at once. We love our animals and feed them well, and look after them. Then they are so full of love and good spirits that they think it is fun to play and work with us."

"I like animals too," said Jimmy. "I would never hurt one, Lotta, so don't look at me like that. One thing I'd like better than any other is a dog of my own — but Dad couldn't possibly buy a licence for him, so I'll never have one! How I wish I belonged to a circus!"

"I wish you belonged too," said Lotta. "Usually in a circus there are lots of children — but I'm the only one here and it's often lonely for me."

"Oh, I say! Look! Who's that over there?" said Jimmy suddenly, pointing to a man who was doing the most extraordinary things on a large mat outside a caravan.

"Oh, that's Oona the acrobat," said Lotta. "He is just

16

practising for tonight. Oona! Here's a friend of mine! Where's your ladder? Do go up it upside down on your hands and stand on your head on the top of it, just to show Jimmy!"

Oona was at that moment looking between his legs at them in a very peculiar manner. He grinned and stood the right way up. "Hallo, youngster!" he said. "So you want to see me do my tricks before you come to the circus!"

"He's not coming," said Lotta. "So do your best trick for him!"

Oona, who was a fine strong-looking young man with a mop of curly golden hair, fetched a step-ladder from his caravan. It was painted gold and looked very grand. Oona stood it firmly on the ground, turned a few somersaults on his mat first, and then walked up the ladder to the very top on his hands, waving his legs above him as he did so.

When he got to the top he stood there on his head alone! Oona lightly twisted himself over and came down beside Jimmy on his feet.

"There!" he said; "easy as winking! Try it yourself!"

"Oh, I couldn't possibly!" said Jimmy. "I can't even walk on my hands."

"*That's* easy, if you like!" said Lotta, and to Jimmy's amazement the little girl flung herself lightly forward and walked a few steps on her hands.

"How I wish *I* could do that!" said Jimmy. "My goodness! The boys at school would stare!"

"Try it," said Lotta. "I'll hold your legs up for you till you get your balance."

Somehow Jimmy got on to his hands and Lotta held his feet up. "Walk on them—walk on your hands!" she shouted. "Go on—I've got your legs all right!"

"I can't!" gasped Jimmy. "I can't make my hands go—my body is so heavy on them!"

Lotta began to laugh. She laughed so much that she dropped Jimmy's legs, and there he was, lying sprawling in the grass, laughing too.

"You'd do for a clown, but not for an acrobat just yet," said Oona, with a grin. "Now off you go—I want to practise!"

"I've got to go and help Lal get into her dress for tonight," said Lotta, as the two children went away. "I must say good-bye, Jimmy. Come again tomorrow."

Jimmy ran off home, his head full of elephants and monkeys and dogs and people standing on their heads and walking on their hands. If only he belonged to a circus too!

JIMMY LEARNS ABOUT
CIRCUS WAYS

Every day Jimmy ran off to the circus field to see Lotta and to hear all her news. She was a lively little girl, kind-hearted but often naughty, and she really could make the most dreadful faces Jimmy had ever seen. She could pinch hard too, and Jimmy didn't like to pinch back.

The circus was doing well. Every night the big tent was crowded with people from the town, and, as it was a very good show, many people went three or four times. Mr. Galliano wore his big top-hat very much on one side of his head, so much so that Jimmy really wondered why it didn't fall off.

"When Galliano wears his hat on one side the circus is taking lots of money," said Lotta to him. "But when you see him wearing it straight up, then you know things are going badly. He gets into a bad temper then, and I hide when I see him coming. I've never seen his hat so much on one side before!"

Jimmy thought that circus ways were very extraordinary. Even hats seemed to share in the excitement! He was afraid of Mr. Galliano, but he couldn't help liking him too. He was such a big handsome man, and his face was so red and his moustache so fierce-looking. He usually carried a whip about with him, and he cracked this very often. It made a noise like a pistol-shot, and Jimmy jumped whenever he heard it. Jimmy made himself a whip with a long string like Mr. Galliano's, but he couldn't make it crack though he tried for a long time.

Jimmy soon knew everybody at the circus. He knew every single one of the dogs. He took them out with Lotta on Saturday morning when there was no school. Lotta had five and he had five. It was hard work keeping the dogs in order. His five kept getting tangled up, but Lotta's never did. The dogs loved Jimmy. How they barked when they saw him!

He gave them their fresh water every day. He even cleaned out their big, airy cage, and put fresh sawdust down. He liked to feel the dogs running round his legs and yapping to him.

Jumbo, the big elephant, was taken down to the nearby stream to drink twice a day. Mr. Tonks untied him and led him down. Jimmy asked if he could lead him back to his tent. Mr. Tonks looked at the little boy.

"What will you do if he runs away from you?" he asked. "Could you catch him by the tail and pull him back? Or would you pick him up and carry him?"

Jimmy laughed. "I guess if he ran away you couldn't bring him back either, Mr. Tonks!" he said. "He won't run away, will he? He's the gentlest creature I ever saw, for all he is so big. Look how he's putting his trunk into my hand now — just as if he wanted me to lead him back."

"Jumbo wouldn't do that if he didn't like you," said Mr. Tonks. "Come on — step on my hand and I'll give you a leg-up, Jimmy. You shall ride on his neck!"

My word! That was a treat for Jimmy! In a trice the little boy was up on the elephant's neck. He sat cross-legged, as Mr. Tonks told him to. The elephant's neck was so broad that this was quite easy. Back went Jimmy and the elephant to the tent. Then, to Jimmy's enormous surprise, the big creature put up his trunk, wound it firmly round his waist, and lifted the boy gently down to the ground himself.

"Oooh!" said Jimmy, astonished. "Thank you, Jumbo!"

"See that!" said Mr. Tonks in surprise. "Jumbo never does that to anyone unless he really likes them. He's your friend for good now, Jimmy. You're lucky!"

After that Jimmy and Jumbo went down to the stream every day together, Jimmy always riding on the elephant's neck. Jimmy saved part of his bread and cheese for Jumbo, and the elephant always looked for it when the boy came to see him. He sometimes put his trunk round Jimmy's neck, and it did feel funny. Like a big snake, Jimmy thought.

There was only one man that Jimmy didn't like – and that was a little, crooked-eyed man called Harry. Harry never had a smile for anyone. He snapped at Lotta, and pulled her hair whenever he passed her. Once Jimmy saw him try to hit Jemima the monkey, when she ran near him.

"I don't like Harry," he said to Lotta. "He has a horrid unkind face. What does he do in the circus, Lotta?"

"He doesn't really belong to us," said the little girl "He's what we call the odd-job man – he does all the odd-jobs – puts up the benches in the ring, mends anything that goes wrong, makes anything special we need. There's always plenty for him to do. He's very clever with his hands – that's why Mr. Galliano keeps him on, but he can't bear him really."

"I saw him try to hit Jemima just now," said Jimmy.

"I've seen him try, too," said Lotta. "But Jemima knows Harry all right. She hates him – do you know, she went to his box of nails one day and stuffed her cheeks with about fifty of his nails. He couldn't find them anywhere – and there was Jemima running about with them in her mouth! I saw her taking them, and I had to hide so that Harry shouldn't see me laughing!"

Jimmy laughed. "Good for Jemima!" he said. "Well, it's a pity you have to keep Harry, Lotta. If I were Mr. Galliano I'd send him away – always snapping and snarling like a bad-tempered dog! He threw his hammer at me yesterday."

"Oh, he wouldn't hit you," said Lotta. "He's too bad

a shot for that. You keep out of his way, though, Jimmy. However much we dislike him we've got to have him — why, we couldn't put up the circus tents and ring without him — and he's so clever at making special ladders and things — and mending caravans."

Just then Mr. Galliano came up, his hat more on one side than ever. He beamed at Jimmy. He had heard that the little boy was marvellous with the animals, and that always pleased Mr. Galliano. He loved every creature, down to white mice, and Lotta had told Jimmy that once, when one of his horses was ill, Mr. Galliano had sat up with her for four nights running and hadn't gone to sleep at all.

"Hallo, boy," he said. "So here you are again! You will be sorry when we move away? Yes?"

"Very sorry," said Jimmy. "I think a circus life is fine!"

"You do not like to live in a house? No?" said Mr. Galliano, who had a very funny way of always putting yes or no at the end of his sentences.

"I'd rather live in a caravan," said Jimmy.

"And you like my circus? Yes?" said Mr. Galliano, twisting his enormous moustache into even sharper points.

"I haven't seen the *real* circus," said Jimmy. "I haven't the money to go into the big tent at night, Mr. Galliano. But I've seen all the animals and people here in the field."

"What! This boy hasn't seen our circus show, the best in the whole world?" cried Mr. Galliano, his big black eyebrows going right up under his curly hair. "He must come, Lotta, he must come tonight! Yes?"

"I'd love to," said Jimmy, red with excitement. "Thanks!"

"Give this to the man at the gate," said Mr. Galliano, and he gave Jimmy a card on which was printed Mr. Galliano's own name. "I shall see you in the big tent tonight then? Yes? Be sure to get there early!"

"Yes sir," said Jimmy, and stuffed the card into his pocket very carefully. Lotta was pleased. She squeezed Jimmy's arm. "Now you'll see us all in the ring!" she said. "I shall be riding, too, tonight, as it's Saturday. Come early!"

The little boy raced home to dinner. He was tremendously excited. All his school-friends had seen the circus—but he, Jimmy, had a special ticket, one of Mr. Galliano's own cards—and he knew everyone there! He knew all the dogs—he had ridden Jumbo! He had cuddled Jemima the clever little monkey! Ah! He would have a glorious time tonight!

The circus began at eight o'clock and lasted for two hours. Jimmy was at the gate at a quarter-past seven. He gave his card to the man there. He was one of the men who looked after Mr. Galliano's many beautiful horses. He grinned at Jimmy. "You can sit anywhere you like with that card!" he said. "My word! Old Galliano was feeling generous this morning, wasn't he—giving free tickets to shrimps like you!"

"I'm not a shrimp," said Jimmy, offended.

"Well, maybe you're a prawn then," said the ticket man. That was just like circus-folk, Jimmy thought—they always had an answer for everything. Perhaps one day he too would be quick enough to think of funny answers—but, oh dear, by that time the circus would have gone!

The little boy went into the big tent. It was lighted by huge flares. Not many people were there yet. There were a great many benches set all round a big red ring in the middle. Mr. Tonks was spreading sawdust in the ring, whistling loudly.

Jimmy chose a seat right in the very front. He whistled to Mr. Tonks. Mr. Tonks looked up and pretended to be most surprised to see Jimmy there.

23

"Hallo, hallo!" he said, 'has somebody left you a fortune or what! Fancy seeing *you* here — in the best seats too — my word, you *are* throwing your money about!"

"No, I'm not," said Jimmy. "Mr. Galliano gave me a ticket."

The tent filled up with people. By the time eight o'clock came there wasn't an empty seat. Jimmy thought that Mr. Galliano must have taken a lot of money tonight, and he wondered if his hat would keep on, he would wear it so much to one side!

There was a doorway at one end, hung with red curtains. Suddenly these were drawn aside and two trumpets blew loudly.

"Tan-tan-tara! Tan-tan-tara! Tan-tan-tara!"

The circus was going to begin! What fun!

JIMMY SEES THE CIRCUS!

"Tan-tan-tara!" went the trumpets again, and into the ring cantered six beautiful black horses. They ran gracefully round the ring, nose to tail. Mr. Galliano came striding into the ring, dressed in a magnificent black suit, his top-hat well on one side, his long stiff moustache turned up like wire.

He cracked his whip. The horses went a bit faster. Galliano cracked his whip twice. The horses all stopped, turned round quickly — and went cantering round the other way. It was marvellous to watch them. How everyone clapped!

Three of the horses went out. The three that were left went on cantering round the ring. They were thoroughly enjoying themselves. Mr. Galliano shouted out something and a barrel-organ began to play a dance tune.

The three horses were delighted. They all loved music. Mr. Galliano cracked his whip sharply. At once all three horses rose up on their hind legs and began to sway in time to the music. Their coats shone like silk. The whip cracked again. Down they went on all-fours and began to gallop round the ring. Every time the music came to a certain chord the horses turned round and galloped the other way.

Everyone clapped till they could clap no more when the horses went out, and they hadn't finished clapping when Sticky Stanley, the clown, came in. He did look funny. His face was painted white, but his nose and lips were red, and he had big false eyebrows that jerked up and down.

He had a broom in his hand and he began to sweep the

ring — and he fell over the broom. He picked himself up, and found that his legs had got twisted round themselves, so he carefully untwisted them and then found that the broom was twisted up with them. So of course he fell over the broom again, and every one laughed and laughed.

Stanley turned somersaults, walked on his hands, carried a sunshade with one of his feet, went round the ring walking on a great round ball, and made so many jokes that Jimmy had a pain in his side with laughing.

Then came Lal, Lotta's mother, with the ten terrier dogs. How lovely they looked, all running into the ring in excitement, their tails wagging, their barks sounding loudly in the big tent.

There were ten little stools set out in the ring, and Lal patted a nearby stool.

"Up! Up!" she said to a dog, and he neatly jumped up and sat down on his stool. Then each dog jumped up on a stool and there they all sat, their mouths open, their tongues hanging out, their tails wagging.

Lal looked grand. She was dressed in a short, fluffy frock of bright pink, and it sparkled and shone as if it were on fire. She had a bright wreath of flowers in her hair and these shone too. Jimmy thought she looked wonderful. He had only seen her before dressed in an old jersey and skirt — but now she looked like something out of Fairyland!

How clever those dogs were! They played follow-my-leader in a long line, and the leader wound them in and out and in. Not a single dog make a mistake! Then they all sat up and begged, and when Lal threw them a biscuit each, they caught their biscuits one after another and barked sharply once.

Lal ran to the side of the ring and fetched the big round ball that Sticky Stanley the clown had walked on so cleverly.

"Up! Up!" she cried to a dog, and it leapt up on the ball and did just as the clown had done — walked swiftly on the top of it as the ball went round! Lal threw him a biscuit for doing it so well.

Then Judy, the little brown-headed terrier, impatient to do her special trick, jumped down from her stool and ran behind Lal. Lal turned in surprise — for it was not like Judy to leave her stool before the right time.

But Judy had seen the hoops of paper that Lal had ready for her, and she wanted to do her trick and get her share of clapping. So she took hold of a hoop and ran to Lal with it. She put it down at Lal's feet and stood there wagging her tail so fast that it couldn't be seen.

Lal laughed. She picked up the hoop and held it shoulder high. "Jump, Judy, jump then!" she cried.

Light as a feather Judy jumped through the hoop, breaking the thin paper as she did so. Then Lal picked up two paper hoops and held them high up, about two feet apart.

"Jump, Judy, jump!" she cried. And Judy, taking a short run, jumped clean through both hoops. How everyone clapped the clever little dog!

Jimmy's face was red with excitement and happiness. How wonderful the circus folk were in the things they could do, and in their love for their animals! Jimmy watched the ten dogs go happily out with Lal, a forest of wagging tails, and he knew that Lal would see that they all got a good hot meal at once. She loved them and they loved her.

The horses came in again — white ones this time — and who do you suppose came in with them? Why, Lotta! Yes, little Lotta, no longer dressed in her ragged old frock, but in a fairy's dress with long silvery wings on her back! Her dark curls were fluffed out round her head and her long legs had on silvery stockings. She wore a little silver

27

crown on her head and carried a silver wand in her hand.

"It can't be Lotta!" said Jimmy to himself, staring hard. But it was. She waved her wand at him as she passed his seat, and—what else do you suppose she did? She made one of her dreadful faces at him!

Lotta jumped lightly up on to the back of one of the white horses. She sat there without holding on at all with her hands, blowing kisses and waving. The horses had no saddles and no bridles. Lotta couldn't have held on to anything if she had wanted to.

Jimmy watched her, his heart thumping in excitement. Whatever would she do next? She suddenly stood up on a horse's back, and there she stayed, balancing perfectly, whilst the horse cantered round and round the ring.

Jimmy was afraid the little girl would fall off—but Lotta knew she wouldn't! She had ridden horses since she was a baby. Down she went again, sitting, and then up again, this time standing backwards, looking towards the tail of the horse. Everyone thought she was very brave and very clever.

Then in came Laddo, her father, dressed in a tight blue shining suit, with glittering stars sewn all over it. He was much more clever than Lotta. The little girl jumped down when her father came in, and ran to the middle of the ring. Laddo jumped up in her place. He leapt from one horse to another as the three of them cantered round the ring. He stood on his hands as they went, he swung himself from side to side underneath a horse's body—really, the things he did you would hardly believe!

Then Lotta jumped up behind him and the two of them galloped out of the ring together, followed by a thunderstorm of clapping and shouting. Jimmy's hands were quite sore with clapping Lotta. He felt very proud of her.

Jumbo came next, and he was very clever, for he

28

certainly could play cricket extremely well. Mr. Tonks bowled a tennis-ball to him and he hit it every time. Once, to Jimmy's great delight, Jumbo hit the ball straight at him, and by jumping up from his seat Jimmy just managed to catch the ball. And then everybody clapped *him*, and Jumbo said, "Hrrrumph, hrrrumph!" very loudly indeed. Jimmy threw the ball to him and he caught it with his trunk.

The circus went on through the evening. Sticky Stanley the clown came in a great many times and always made everyone laugh, because he seemed to fall over everything, even things that were not there. Lilliput and his monkeys were very clever. They helped Lilliput to set a table with cups and saucers and plates. They got chairs. They sat down at the table. They had feeders tied round their necks, and they passed one another a plate of fruit.

Jemima was the best. She peeled a banana for Lilliput and fed him with it! But then she stuffed the peel down his neck and he pretended to chase her all round the ring, and everyone laughed till they cried.

Then Jemima got into a corner and pretended to cry. When Lilliput came up she took his handkerchief out of his pocket and wiped her eyes with it. Then she leapt on to Lilliput's shoulder and spread the handkerchief over the top of his head. Jimmy laughed just as much at Jemima as he did at the clown.

Of course Oona the acrobat had a lot of clapping too, especially when he walked up his step-ladder on his hands and stood on the top on just his head! Stanley the clown came running in to try and do it, but of course he couldn't, and he fell all the way down the ladder, bumpity-bumpity-bump! Jimmy was afraid he might hurt himself, but he saw Stanley grinning all the time, so he knew he was all right.

Oona did another clever thing too—he had a wire rope

put up from one post to another, and he walked on the rope, which was about as high as Mr. Galliano's top-hat from the ground. Jimmy hadn't known he could do that—and he wondered how Oona did it. Surely it must be very difficult to walk on a rope without falling off at all!

The circus came to an end all too soon. All the circus folk came running into the ring, shouting, bowing, jumping, and everyone clapped them and shouted too.

"Best circus that's ever come to this town!" said a big man next to Jimmy. "Fine show. I shall come and see it next week too. That little girl on horseback was very good—one of the best!"

Jimmy saved that up to tell Lotta. He would see her tomorrow. There was no circus on Sunday. The circus folk had a rest that day, and Lotta had said that Jimmy could spend the day with her.

"I must run straight home now," thought Jimmy to himself. "Mother will be waiting for me. What a lot I shall have to tell her!"

So he ran home, though he would dearly have loved to find the fairy-like Lotta with her silvery wings and talked to her.

A SHOCK FOR MR. GALLIANO

It was Sunday. Jimmy remembered that he was to spend the whole day with Lotta. What fun it would be to wander about amongst the circus folk and see old Jumbo, and pet Jemima the clever little monkey, and have his hands licked by all the jolly little terrier dogs! Jimmy sang loudly as he got up.

He was soon in the circus field. The sun shone down. It was going to be a lovely day. But as he made his way between the caravans and the tents Jimmy saw that everyone looked gloomy.

"I wonder what the matter is?" thought Jimmy to himself. He passed the clown's caravan, and saw Sticky Stanley eating a breakfast of bacon and eggs. Stanley looked miserable. It was strange to see the clown looking like that.

He saw Jimmy and called out to him: "Hey, Jimmy, don't you let Mr. Galliano see you this morning! He's forbidden any outsiders to come into the circus field."

"Why?" asked Jimmy, in astonishment. "He was very nice to me yesterday. He gave me a ticket. What's the matter?"

"Listen to that, then!" said the clown, pointing with his fork towards the big blue caravan in which Mr. Galliano lived with his wife. "Just listen to that!"

Jimmy listened. It sounded as if about six cows were bellowing in Galliano's caravan — but it was only Mr. Galliano being very angry indeed, and shouting at the top of his very big voice. Jimmy stared in the direction of the blue caravan — and as he stared, Mr. Galliano came down the steps at the back.

31

"He's got his hat on quite straight up," said Jimmy, at once. "He's always had it on one side before."

"Yes, that means bad news, all right," said the clown. "Hop off, Jimmy. Don't let him see you."

Jimmy hopped off. He ran round the clown's caravan and came to the red-and-white one in which Lotta lived with Lal and Laddo, her mother and father. Lotta was sitting on the steps outside, polishing her circus shoes.

"Hallo, Jimmy," she said. "Come up here."

"Lotta, what's the matter with everyone this morning?" asked Jimmy. "You all look so gloomy, and I just heard Mr. Galliano in a bad temper."

"There's matter enough," said Lotta, dropping her voice. "You know Harry, our odd-job man — the carpenter who puts up the benches, does most of the packing and unpacking and all the little mending and making jobs a circus always has? Well — he ran away last night, taking nearly all the money with him that the circus took last week!"

"Oh, I say, how dreadful!" said Jimmy, shocked. "Won't you get any money, then?"

"Not a penny," said Lotta. "And that's very hard, you know, because we none of us save anything. The worst of it is, Harry was so useful — we don't really know how we are going to do without him."

"Perhaps he will be caught," said Jimmy.

"I don't think so," said Lotta. "He had a good start, because he took the money when we were all asleep last night and went off about two o'clock in the morning. He may be anywhere now. I do hope we have a good week now, Jimmy — if we don't, it will be very bad for us all."

"I hope you do too," said Jimmy. "I wish I could help, Lotta."

"I suppose you don't know a good handy carpenter in your town who could come along for a week and help us, do you?" said Lal, Lotta's mother, coming to the door of the caravan. "There are a lot of jobs that must be done before tomorrow night. Oona's ladder must be made stronger, he says. And there's a bar loose in the dogs' big cage."

"What about my father?" said Jimmy eagerly. "He's a carpenter, you know! He could do anything you wanted!"

"Yes, but what about his work?" said Lal. "He can't leave that to come to us."

"He's out of work," said Jimmy. "He would be glad to come. Oh, Lotta—will you come to tea with me at home today and we could find out if my father will come? I do, do hope he can."

"We'd better tell Mr. Galliano first," said Lal. She called to her husband at the back of the caravan: "Laddo, will you go and tell Galliano about his father being a carpenter?"

"Right," said Laddo. He put down his newspaper and ran down the caravan steps with Jimmy. "Come on, son," he said.

Mr. Galliano, who was with his horses, heard Jimmy and Laddo coming and he turned to meet them.

"What do you want?" he said, not at all pleased to see Jimmy.

"Mr. Galliano, sir, this boy says his father is a carpenter and could take Harry's place for the week," said Laddo.

"Tell him to come and see me this evening, yes," said Mr. Galliano shortly, and he turned back to his horses and talked gently to them.

No matter how bad a temper he sometimes flew into, he never was anything but gentle with his beloved horses. No one had ever seen him sharp or unkind with any animal. All his horses loved him and would do anything for him.

Laddo and Jimmy went out. Jimmy felt excited. Just

suppose his father got the job to help the circus—and just suppose they kept him on! Oh, wouldn't that be wonderful!

He ran back to Lotta. "Let's go for a walk with the dogs," said Jimmy. "It's such a lovely day—and everyone is so gloomy here this morning. We can get back here to dinner."

"All right," said Lotta, and the two ran to get the excited terriers. Soon Lotta had five of the dogs on her big lead, and Jimmy had the other five. Lotta was a little bit jealous because all the dogs seemed to want to go with Jimmy.

"I never saw anyone so good with animals as you, Jimmy," she said. "At least, that's not counting Mr. Galliano—he can tame a wild tiger and make it purr like a cat in two days!"

The two children set off over the countryside. In a little while Lotta forgot about Harry and how he had run off with everyone's money. Soon the two were having great fun, racing with their dogs and joining in the barking with laughs and shrieks.

"Shall we let them loose for a real good run?" asked Jimmy, when they were well out in the country. "They would love it so!" So they let all the dogs loose, and with excited yaps the neat little terriers tore off to go rabbiting. Jimmy and Lotta sat under a tree.

"I did love the circus last night, Lotta," said Jimmy. "And I did think you were clever—riding on a horse standing up and never falling off!"

"Pooh," said Lotta, making a face at him. "That's easy. You could do it yourself."

"I couldn't," said Jimmy. "I can't even walk on my hands yet, and it does look so easy when you all do it! I wish you'd teach me, Lotta."

"All right," said Lotta. "But not now. I'm too hot. I

wish you belonged to the circus, Jimmy. I shall be lost without you. It's nice to have someone to make faces at when I feel like it."

"I can't think why you want to do that," said Jimmy, surprised. "All the same — I'd like to go with you when you go off again. But I wouldn't like to leave my mother and father."

"Where are those dogs?" said Lotta suddenly. "We mustn't lose any, you know, Jimmy. My word, we should get into trouble if we did! Hie, Judy, Darky, Nigger, Spot!"

Some of the dogs came running up and flung themselves on the two children. Jimmy counted them. "Eight," he said. "Where are the others?"

They quickly put the eight dogs on the leads. Lotta looked worried. "Whistle, Jimmy," she said. So Jimmy whistled.

"There comes Punch!" said Lotta, and sure enough one of the missing dogs came loping over the field towards them. Jimmy whistled again and again—but the tenth dog was nowhere to be seen!

"We shall have to go," said Lotta, looking scared. "Whatever will Lal and Laddo say when we turn up without Darky? Come on—it's getting late. Perhaps Darky will come after us when he's finished hunting."

They went back to the circus. No Darky came after them. Lotta was very silent. Jimmy was miserable too. What a horrid day this was after all!"

"We'll put the dogs into the cage, and then we'll go and tell Lal we've lost Darky," said Lotta. She was crying now. Lotta loved all the dogs and she couldn't help wondering if Darky had been caught in a trap. Also she knew that her mother would be very angry with her.

Jimmy opened the door of the great cage. As he did so a little dark dog crept out from under the cage itself. Jimmy gave a yell.

"Lotta! Darky's here! He must have run all the way home before us and hidden under his cage. Look!"

Lotta gave a shriek of delight and hugged Darky. "You silly animal!" she said. "You did give me a fright! Oh, Jimmy—I'm so happy now!"

Jimmy was glad. He squeezed Lotta's hand as they ran to the caravan for dinner. Lotta squeezed his hand back —but she was so strong that she made Jimmy yell out in pain. You never knew what that little monkey of a Lotta was going to do next! Jimmy dropped her hand in a hurry and felt half-cross with her. But when he smelt the smell of frying sausages he forgot everything except that he was dreadfully hungry.

They all had their dinner sitting outside the caravan. The sausages were lovely and so were the potatoes cooked in their jackets and eaten with butter and salt. Jimmy thought he had never had such a lovely dinner in his life. Afterwards there were oranges and chocolate to eat.

Jimmy took Lotta home to tea with him. He ran indoors with the little girl and found his mother making toast for tea. They always had toast on Sundays. It smelt good.

"Mother, this is Lotta. I've brought her home to tea because I want to ask Dad something. Where is he?"

"Out in the garden, mending the old shed," said Mother. "Hallo, Lotta! How's the circus going?"

"All right, thank you," said Lotta shyly. She looked at Jimmy's mother and thought she was lovely. She was so neat and her face was so kind. Lotta had not often been inside a house, and she looked round curiously. It seemed just as strange to her to be inside a house as it was to Jimmy to be inside a caravan.

"Dad! Dad!" shouted Jimmy, running into the back garden. "Harry, the odd-job man at the circus, has run off with the circus money—and Mr. Galliano wants a new carpenter. He says will you go and see him tonight."

"That's the first bit of luck I've had for a long time," said Jimmy's father, delighted. "Yes, I'll go up and see if I can get the work after tea. A week's work is better than nothing. Well, that's given me an appetite for my tea! Is the toast ready, Mother?"

Soon Lotta, Jimmy, and the two grown-ups were sitting round the tea-table. Lotta was on her very best behaviour. She didn't make a single face. She liked Jimmy's mother much too much to shock her!

After tea, Jimmy, Lotta, and Jimmy's father set off to the circus field. "If only I can get that job!" said Jimmy's father.

"I *do* hope you do, Dad!" said Jimmy.

AN EXCITING NIGHT

Jimmy, Lotta, and Jimmy's father soon got to the circus field. "There's Mr. Galliano, over there," said Lotta, as they went through the gate.

"Right," said Mr. Brown. "I'll go over and see him now." He left the two children and walked over to where Mr. Galliano was talking to Oona the acrobat.

"What do you want?" said Mr. Galliano, seeing that Mr. Brown was a stranger.

"I'm Jimmy Brown's father," said Mr. Brown. "I'm a carpenter, sir, and I can turn my hand to anything. I'd like you to give me a chance, if you will. I'd work well for you."

Mr. Galliano looked Mr. Brown up and down. He liked what he saw—a strong, kindly-faced man, with bright eager eyes just like Jimmy's.

"Come tomorrow morning," said Mr. Galliano. "There will be plenty for you to do, yes!"

"Thank you, sir," said Mr. Brown, and he walked off, pleased. It would be fine to work at last! The two children ran to meet him. How glad Jimmy was to know that his father would belong to the circus for at least a week! What would the boys at school say when they knew that his father was with the circus all day? They would think that was fine!

Jimmy's father worked well. Mr. Galliano was delighted with him. He could, as he said, turn his hand to anything. He mended five of the circus benches. He put a new wheel on to Mr. Galliano's caravan. He made Oona's ladder stronger than it had ever been before. He put in two new bars where the dogs had pushed them loose in their cage.

And he won Lilliput's heart by making him a proper little house for Jemima the monkey to live in—it even had a little door!

Jimmy was delighted to hear everyone praising his father. He had always loved his father and thought him the finest man in the world—and it was nice to hear people saying he was ten times better than Harry!

"His laugh is worth ten shillings a week!" said Lal. "My, when old Brownie starts laughing, you've got to hold your sides!"

Jimmy thought it was funny to hear his father called Brownie. But the circus folk hardly ever called anyone by their right name. Brownie was the name they gave to Mr. Brown, and Brownie he always was, after that!

The circus did well again that week. Mr. Galliano began to wear his hat on the side of his head once more. Everyone cheered up. If Galliano was merry and bright, then the circus folk were happy.

Jimmy was happy too that week. He had to go to school, but every spare minute he had he was in the circus field, helping. He was always ready to give a hand to anyone. When the circus show began each night, Jimmy stood near the curtains through which the performers had to pass, and pulled or shut the curtains properly each time. He got Oona's ladder and tight-rope ready for him. He took care of the dogs whilst they were waiting for their turn. He got Jumbo out of his tent too, for Mr. Tonks, and took him back again when the show was over. Jumbo loved Jimmy. He blew gently down the little boy's neck to show him how much he liked him. Jimmy thought that was very funny!

When Saturday came, Mr. Galliano whistled to Mr. Brown—or Brownie, as he was now called—and Brownie went to him.

"Here's your week's money," said Mr. Galliano, paying

him. "Now look here—you've done well—what about you coming along with us, yes? We can do with a man like you—always cheerful, and able to do anything that turns up."

Mr. Brown went red with pleasure. It was a long time since anyone had praised him.

"Thank you, sir," he said. "I'll have to talk it over with my wife. You see—I think she would be upset if I left her and Jimmy. I might not see them again for a long time."

"Well, think over it," said Mr. Galliano. "If you come, you can live with Stanley, the clown. He's got room in his caravan. We go off tomorrow—so let me know quickly, yes?"

Mr. Brown hurried home to dinner. He told Jimmy and Jimmy's mother all that Mr. Galliano had said.

"I think I'll have to take the job," he said. "It's hard to leave you both, though."

Jimmy's mother didn't know what to say. She couldn't help the tears coming into her eyes.

"Oh, Tom," said his mother, "I shall miss you so. Don't go. I can't bear to be without you—and Jimmy will miss you so much too. We shall never know where you are, travelling about the country—and goodness knows when we shall see you again!"

"Well, we needn't tell Mr. Galliano till tomorrow," said Mr. Brown. "We'll talk about it tonight."

Jimmy thought and thought about it. He badly wanted his father to belong to the circus—but not if he and his mother had to be left behind! No—that would never do at all! And yet they couldn't go with him. There wasn't room for them. And if his father said no to Mr. Galliano then he might be out of work again for a long long time—just as he had found a job that he could do so well.

It was a puzzle to know what to do. Jimmy felt that he

really, really, couldn't bear it if his father had to leave home. His mother would be so sad.

The circus gave its last show that night. It did very well, and once again there was not an empty seat in the big tent, for people came from all the towns round to see it. Somebody gave Lotta a big box of chocolates and she was very pleased. She showed them to Jimmy. "We'll share them," she said, emptying out half the box into a bag. "They're lovely."

That was just like Lotta. She was the most generous little girl that Jimmy had ever known. But Jimmy could not smile very much at her. The circus was going off the next day to a far away town. He would have to say good-bye. He felt as if he had known the circus folk all his life, and he was sad to part with them.

"I'll come and see you tomorrow morning, Lotta," he said.

"Come early," said Lotta. "We'll be packing up to go, and that is a busy time. We shall start off about twelve o'clock. We've got to get to Edgingham by night."

"Good-night then," said Jimmy, looking at Lotta hard, so as to remember for always just how she looked — she had on her fluffy circus frock, her long silver wings, her little silver crown, and her silvery stockings. As he looked at her she made one of her dreadful faces!

"Don't!" said Jimmy. "I was just thinking how nice you looked."

"You'd better hurry home," said Lotta. "It looks as if a storm is coming up. Hark! That's thunder!"

Jimmy ran off. Certainly there was a storm coming. Great drops of rain fell on him as he ran through the town and stung his face. The thunder rolled nearer. A flash of lightning lit up the sky, and Jimmy saw that it was full of enormous black clouds, hanging very low.

Jimmy's mother was glad to see him, for she had been

afraid he would be caught in the storm. She bundled him into bed and he fell asleep almost at once, for he was tired.

The storm crashed on. Jimmy slept peacefully and didn't hear it. Away up in the circus field the folk there listened to the pouring rain pattering down on their caravans.

Crash! The thunder rolled again. The horses whinnied, half-frightened. The dogs awoke and barked. Jemima, the monkey, who always slept with Lilliput, crept nearer to him and began to cry like a child. Lilliput petted her gently.

Jumbo, the big elephant, raised his great head. What was this fearful noise that was going on around him? Jumbo was angry with it. He threw back his head and trumpeted loudly to frighten it away.

Crash! Crash! The thunder still rolled on, and one crash sounded just overhead. Jumbo, half-angry, half-frightened, pulled at his post. His leg was tied to it, but in a trice the big elephant had snapped the thick rope. He blundered out of the tent, looking for the one man he trusted above everybody—his keeper, Mr. Tonks.

But Mr. Tonks was fast asleep in his caravan. Not even a storm could keep Mr. Tonks awake. He snored in his caravan as if he were trying to beat the loudness of the thunder!

Jumbo grew frightened in the dark. He stood in the rain, waving his big ears to and fro and swinging his trunk backwards and forwards. Another peal of thunder broke through the night, and a flash of lightning showed the gate to Jumbo. It was open.

The elephant, remembering that he had come in through that gate, made his way towards it. No one heard him, for the rolling of the thunder and the pattering of the rain made such a noise. Jumbo slipped through the gate

42

like a great black shadow, and set off alone up the lane that led to the town.

No one was about except Mr. Harris, the town policeman. He was sheltering from the rain in a doorway. He got a dreadful shock when he saw Jumbo lit up in a flash of lightning, coming up the street towards him. He didn't know it was only Jumbo. He fled away as fast as he could back to the police-station. He was the only person who met Jumbo running away.

The storm passed. The rain stopped. The night became peaceful and everyone slept. The circus dogs lay down and Jemima the monkey stopped crying.

The morning broke peaceful and bright, though the circus field was soaking wet.

Mr. Tonks dressed himself and went straight out to see his beloved Jumbo. When he looked into the tall tent and saw no elephant there, he went white.

"Jumbo! Where's my elephant!" he shouted, and he tore all round the field, waking everyone up. Heads peeped out of caravans and scared faces looked up and down.

"Jumbo's gone! My elephant's gone!" cried Mr. Tonks, tears pouring down his cheeks. "Where is he, where is he?"

"Well, he's not in anybody's caravan, that's certain," said Stanley, the clown. "Can't you see his tracks anywhere, Tonky?"

"Yes—they lead out of the gate!" said Mr. Tonks, almost off his head with shock and grief. "What's happened to him? I'll let the police know. He must be found before anything happens to him."

"Well, he's too big to lose for long," said Mr. Galliano, coming out of his caravan with his hat on the side of his head. "Don't worry, Tonks. We'll soon find him."

But somebody already knew where Jumbo had gone— and who do you suppose that was? It was Jimmy!

In the middle of the storm Jimmy awoke suddenly.

He sat up in bed, looking puzzled. He had heard a funny noise outside his house. It sounded like "Hrrrumph! Hrrrumph!" Who made a noise like that? Jumbo, of course!

"But it can't be Jumbo," said Jimmy, in the greatest astonishment. He hopped out of bed and ran to the window. A flash of lightning lit up the little street—and quite clearly Jimmy saw Jumbo, plodding heavily up the street towards the town!

"It *is* Jumbo—and he's frightened of the storm—and has run away!" thought Jimmy. "I must go after him!"

He dragged on his coat, put his feet into his shoes at the same time, and slipped downstairs. In a trice he was out of the house and running up the street after Jumbo. He must get him, he must! Poor old Jumbo, running away all alone, frightened of the storm!

"Jumbo, Jumbo!" called Jimmy—but Jumbo padded on.

JIMMY HUNTS FOR JUMBO

Jimmy rushed up the street, calling Jumbo. The thunder rolled round and every now and again a flash of lightning showed him the big elephant padding through the streets. Jumbo could go very fast indeed when he liked and Jimmy couldn't catch up with him. "If only I can keep him in sight," panted Jimmy to himself. "Jumbo! Can't you hear me shouting to you? Jumbo! Come to Jimmy!"

Jumbo took no notice at all. He went round the corner. He lumbered up the next street and the next. He came to the market-square and crossed it. Jimmy panted and puffed a good way behind him, pleased when the lightning lighted the night and showed him where Jumbo was.

Jumbo came to the better part of the town where the roads were wider, and where the houses were large, with big gardens. He padded along, his great feet making very little sound. Pad-pad-pad he went through the night, his big ears twitching and his little tail swinging. His trunk was curled up safely, for Jumbo was afraid that the thunder and lightning might harm it. Sometimes he gave a loud "hrrumph!" and then the people in the houses nearby sat up in alarm and wondered whatever the strange noise was!

The elephant left the town behind. Beyond lay the woods, sloping up a big hill. Jumbo was pleased to come to trees and grass. He plodded on right into the wood and climbed half-way up the hill. Jimmy still followed him — and then he lost him!

It happened like this — the storm suddenly died down, and the lightning stopped. Jimmy could no longer see the elephant in the flashes, and as the wood was thick it was difficult to know which way Jumbo went now that he was not going down a road. Jimmy stopped and listened. Far away he could hear something crashing through the bushes—he knew it was Jumbo, but he could not tell which way to go to find him.

"Oh dear," said the little boy, terribly disappointed. "I've come all this way and I haven't found Jumbo after all!"

He stood there by himself in the dark woods, wondering what to do. And then he suddenly saw a little light shining through the trees! He stared at it in surprise.

"What can that light be from?" he wondered. He made his way towards it, feeling before him as he went, for he did not want to walk into trees. It was dark and everywhere was wet. Jimmy shivered. He wished he were back in his own warm bed!

Stumbling over bushes and roots he came at last to the light. It shone from a cottage window. The blind was not drawn and Jimmy could see inside the room. He peeped in at the window.

A man was in the room, dressed in a gamekeeper's coat and leggings. He was bending over a dog that lay in a basket. The dog was ill, and one of its legs was bandaged. The man was stroking it and saying something to it, though Jimmy could not hear a word.

"He looks a kind man," thought the little boy. "Perhaps he will let me come in and dry my clothes." So Jimmy knocked gently at the window.

The gamekeeper looked up at once, in the greatest astonishment, for it was the middle of the night. He walked to the window and opened it.

"Who's there?" he said.

"It's me, Jimmy Brown," said Jimmy, the light shining on his face. "I came to look for Jumbo, the elephant, but I've lost him, and I'm so wet I thought perhaps you'd let me come in and dry my clothes."

The gamekeeper stared as if he couldn't believe his ears.

"What nonsense are you talking?" he said. "Looking for an elephant—an *elephant*! Whatever do you mean?"

"It's Jumbo, the circus elephant," said Jimmy, and he was going on to explain everything when the keeper told him to go to the door and come inside.

The little boy was glad to get into the cottage. The gamekeeper listened to his story in surprise. Then he felt Jimmy's coat, which he had thrown on over his pyjamas.

"I'll make a fire here," said the man. "You'll get a terrible chill if you keep those wet clothes on any longer. It's a mercy you found me up. My dear old dog, Flossie, got knocked down by a car this morning and I'm sitting up with her tonight to make sure she's all right. Else I should have been in bed."

He made Jimmy take off his wet things and put on a coat and dressing-gown of his. They were much too big for Jimmy, but they were dry. The man lighted a fire on the hearth and soon there was a cheerful crackling of wood. Jimmy sat drowsily by the fire, drinking hot cocoa and feeling suddenly very sleepy.

"I do wish I could have found Jumbo," he said. "I don't know how I can find him now. Mr. Tonks, his keeper, will be so upset."

"Don't you worry about finding elephants," said the man. "I can track a baby rabbit if I want to—and you may be sure that Jumbo will leave tracks quite plain to see! We'll go hunting for him in the morning!"

"But I must go home tonight," began Jimmy—and then somehow his eyes closed, his head nodded, and he was fast asleep in the keeper's chair by the blazing fire!

He didn't wake up till morning. He heard the gamekeeper moving about and opened his eyes. Breakfast was on the table! There was porridge, bread and marmalade, and hot cocoa. It looked good to Jimmy.

The man had put him on a sofa in the corner, still wearing his large coat and dressing-gown. But now Jimmy's own clothes were dry and he put them on, chattering to the kind keeper all the time, and really feeling most excited. They were going to find Jumbo after breakfast!

"How is your dog Flossie?" asked Jimmy, patting the sleek head of the big spaniel in the basket.

"Better," said the keeper. "I think her leg will heal all right. I'll leave her in her basket this morning with some milk nearby, and she'll sleep and be all right. If it hadn't been for Flossie you wouldn't have seen a light shining in my cottage last night, young man!"

"I know," said Jimmy, stroking the dog, who lifted her pretty head and gave Jimmy a feeble lick with her tongue. "Good dog, Flossie! Get better soon! Good dog, then!"

"You're good with animals," said the Keeper watching Jimmy. "Flossie hates strangers — you're the first one she has ever licked."

Soon after breakfast things were cleared away and the two of them slipped out-of-doors into the wet woods. The sun was shining, the birds were singing, and everywhere was golden. It was a beautiful May day.

"Look! That's where Jumbo passed last night," said Jimmy, pointing to where some bushes were trampled down. "We can follow his track from there."

"Come along, then," said the keeper. So the two of them followed Jumbo's track. It was not at all difficult, for the elephant had made a real pathway for himself through the wood.

"Look! Jumbo pulled up a whole tree there!" said Jimmy in surprise. He pointed to where a birch tree lay uprooted. How strong he was!

"Elephants can easily pull up trees," said the keeper. "Come on—the track goes over to the right just here."

They went on and on through the wood, up the side of the hill—and quite suddenly they were upon Jumbo! He was lying down beneath a thick oak tree, his ears flapping to and fro, and his little eyes watching to see who was coming.

"Jumbo! Dear old Jumbo! I've found you at last!" cried Jimmy, and he ran up to the big animal and stroked his long trunk. Jumbo trumpeted loudly. He was pleased to see Jimmy. He was no longer frightened, for the storm had gone—but he felt strange and queer by himself in a quiet wood, instead of in the noisy circus field, with all his friends round him. He got to his feet and ran his trunk round Jimmy lovingly.

The gamekeeper stood a little way off, looking on in surprise. He was half afraid of the enormous elephant—but Jumbo took no notice of him at all. He had got his friend Jimmy and that was all he cared!

"Jumbo, you must come back to the circus field with me," said Jimmy, stroking him. "Mr. Tonks will be looking for you."

"Hrrumph!" said Jumbo, when he heard Mr. Tonks's name. He adored his keeper. He put his trunk round Jimmy's waist and lifted him up on to his neck. But Jimmy cried out to him to take him down again.

"Jumbo, let me down! If you take me through the trees on your back the branches will sweep me off! You are so tall, you know. Let me walk beside you through the woods and when we come to the town I'll ride."

Jumbo understood. He lifted Jimmy down again, and then the two of them started off through the woods, down the hill towards the town. Jimmy called good-bye to the kind gamekeeper, who was staring at them in wonder, and very soon the two were out of sight.

After a while the woods came to an end and Jimmy walked beside Jumbo up a lane. Jumbo stopped and looked down at Jimmy. "Hrrumph?" he said gently.

Jimmy understood. "Yes, you can carry me now," he said. "We can go more quickly then."

Jumbo lifted him up on to his head. Jimmy crossed his legs and sat there. Jumbo set off at a good pace down the lane and into a big road. He knew the way back quite well, although he had only been there once, the night before.

People looked up when they heard the big elephant padding along—and *how* they stared when they saw Jimmy on the elephant! They ran after him, pointing and shouting in surprise and amazement.

"It's the elephant that was lost! Look, it's the circus elephant!" they cried.

Through the market-place went Jimmy, feeling tremendously proud, for really he was making a great disturbance and everyone seemed most astonished. Jumbo padded on to the circus field—and there he and Jimmy were met by the whole of the circus folk, Mr. Galliano and Mr. Tonks at the front, Mr. Tonks yelling himself hoarse with delight to see his beloved elephant safely back again!

Jimmy had to tell his tale over and over again. Mr. Tonks flung his arms round him and hugged him till Jimmy felt as if his bones were breaking. The elephant's keeper was quite mad with joy and delight. Tears poured down his cheeks as he stroked Jumbo's trunk, and the big elephant stood trumpeting in joy to see his keeper again. Everyone was excited and pleased.

And in the middle of it all, Mr. Galliano, his hat well on one side, suddenly made a most surprising speech!

"Jimmy Brown!" he began. "You are a most remarkable boy—yes? You love animals and they love you—you should live with them and care for them. Yes? Very well. We will take you and your father with us, both of you, and if your mother will come too, then we will have your whole family, and it will not be too much for us. No? You shall belong to the circus — yes, no, yes?"

Mr. Galliano got quite muddled, he was so pleased and excited. As for Jimmy he was almost off his head with delight. Belong to the circus? Go off with them — and Lotta! Oh, what joy! The very thing he would like best in all the world.

"I must go and tell my mother!" he said, and he ran off home at top speed!

JIMMY JOINS THE CIRCUS

Jimmy tore home to tell his mother all the adventures of the night — and to ask her if she would go with the circus. Then Dad would have a job, and he, Jimmy, would be able to help with the animals, and Mother would be with them to care for them and love them. Nobody would have to be left behind.

His mother and father were looking very worried when he got home, for they had found his bed empty that morning and hadn't known where he had gone. And what had puzzled them more than ever was to find that he had left his trousers behind! Wherever could he have gone in his pyjamas?

Jimmy soon told them all about how he had gone to find Jumbo in the middle of the night — and how he had spent the night at the gamekeeper's cottage — and they had looked for Jumbo in the morning. His parents listened in amazement.

"But listen, Mum—listen, Dad," said Jimmy. "I've got something much more wonderful to tell you! Mr. Galliano wants *me* to go off with the circus—to help with the animals! What do you think of that? And he says you can go too, Mother—and Dad will be the odd-job man and do everything that is needed in a travelling circus!"

His mother and father stared at Jimmy as if he had gone quite mad. Then his mother began to cry, quite suddenly. She wiped her eyes with her handkerchief and said, "I'm not really crying. I'm happy to think your father's got a good job at last—and you're quite a hero, Jimmy darling—and I can go with you both and look after you."

"Mother, then you'll come?" shouted Jimmy, jumping up and down in joy, and flinging his arms first round his father and then round his mother. "We'll all be together. Oh, that will be glorious."

"Yes—but what about a caravan?" said his father. "We can't all share the clown's caravan, you know. That would have been all right for me—but not for you two as well."

"We'll ask Mr. Galliano about that," said Jimmy. "He's a wonderful man, I'll go right away now. Mother, can you pack today and come?"

"Jimmy! Of course not!" said his mother, looking round at her bits of furniture.

"Oh, Mother, you must!" said Jimmy. "You won't want much in a caravan, really you won't. I'll get Lotta's father and mother to come along and tell you what to take."

The excited boy rushed off to the circus field. He was singing for joy. First he must find Lotta and tell her the great news. He saw her with five of the dogs.

"Lotta, Lotta!" he yelled. "I've got news for you! *I'm* going to join the circus too."

Lotta was so surprised and delighted that she dropped the dogs' lead and all the dogs scampered off in different directions. The two children spent ten minutes getting them back, and then Jimmy told Lotta everything. She listened joyfully, and then gave Jimmy a big pinch.

"I can't help pinching you, I feel so glad!" she said.

"Well, it's a funny way of showing you're glad," said poor Jimmy, rubbing his arm. "But you're a funny girl altogether, Lotta—more like a boy—so I don't mind much—I don't mind anything today, because I'm joining the circus, the circus, the circus!"

"He's joining our circus, circus, circus!" shouted Lotta, and she threw herself over on to her hands and turned cart-wheel somersaults all round the field. That made Jimmy laugh. It always looked so easy and was so dreadfully difficult when *he* tried to do it!

He went to find Mr. Galliano. Mr. Galliano was so pleased that Jumbo had been found and brought back safely that his hat was almost falling off, it was so much on one side. He was glad to see Jimmy again.

"You are coming with us—yes?" he cried, and banged Jimmy on the back.

"Yes, Mr. Galliano," said Jimmy, his brown eyes shining brightly. "But we haven't a caravan, you know. How can we manage it?"

"Easy, easy!" said Mr. Galliano. "We have an old small caravan that is used for storing things in. We will take them out, and put them into an empty cage for now. Your mother can clean out the old caravan and you can all come in that! Yes? But we go today, Jimmy, we go today! Is that your father I see over there—yes!"

It was. "Good-day, sir," said Mr. Brown, smiling at Jimmy, who was capering round in delight. "We'll all come with you, sir."

Mr. Galliano took Mr. Brown to the old caravan and

told him he could have it, if he would store the things inside it into an empty cage they had. Mr. Brown listened. He turned to Jimmy.

"Go back to your mother and tell her all this," he said. "Take Lotta with you. She may be able to help."

"We will not start till two hours later than usual, yes?" said Mr. Galliano generously. "That will give you and your family time to get everything ready."

My goodness, what a day that was! Jimmy, Lotta, and Lotta's mother, Lal, went rushing off to Jimmy's home to help his mother. Lal was a great help. She looked quickly round the bare little house and said at once what was to go and what was to be sold. She found a man who would buy the things that were not wanted. She helped to take down the curtains. She said that the frying-pans must certainly all be taken — and the big kettle — and the oil-stove for cooking — and the little stool — but only one chair. The big bed could go into the caravan, for it was not a very large size and Jimmy would have to sleep on a mattress at night, in a corner of the caravan.

It did sound exciting. Lotta said they must take their two candlesticks, and a little folding-table. The iron must be taken, for circus clothes must always be fresh and stiffly ironed. The wash-tub could hang under the caravan. Jimmy entered into everything, and was so thrilled to think he would sleep on a mattress only and not on a bed that he could hardly stop dancing around.

"Jimmy, you are more hindrance than help," said his mother at last. "Go to your father and ask him if he can bring the caravan down to the house as soon as possible, for we can easily put the things into it here."

Off went Jimmy and Lotta, rushing at top speed. Neither of them could walk that day, things were too exciting! They found Mr. Brown. He had stored all the things from the old caravan into an empty cage, and had given it a rough clean. It was a small and rather ugly old caravan, badly in need of paint—but to Jimmy's eyes it was beautiful! It was a home on wheels, and what more could a little boy want?

He went to fetch one of the circus horses to take the caravan down to his house. Soon there was great excitement in Jimmy's street when the neighbours learnt what was happening. "The Browns are going off with the circus!" people shouted to one another, and they came to help. Lal scrubbed the floor of the old caravan for Jimmy's mother. Lotta cleaned the windows. There were four— two little ones at the front and one at each side. There

was a door at the back and the usual little ladder hanging down.

The carpet was put down. It was the one out of Jimmy's little bedroom, for the other carpets were too big for the small caravan. No curtains fitted the windows, so those would have to be put up later. The stove was put in its corner. The bed was put in, but not put up. There wasn't time for that. In went the one chair and the little stool, the frying-pans, and the kettle and all the rest.

In the middle of it all Lotta, who had gone back to help her own mother pack up, came flying down the road. "Jimmy! Jimmy! We're off! Oh, do hurry! Don't get left behind!"

The last few things were bundled into the old caravan. Jimmy waved good-bye and ran up the steps. His father sat on the front and clicked to the horse. His mother shut the door of her house for the last time and ran down the path, half laughing and half crying. The neighbours kissed her and wished her luck.

"Good-bye, good-bye!" they cried. "We'll come and see you all when next the circus comes here. Good-bye!"

The horse trotted down the street, with Lotta riding on its back, and Mr. Brown holding the reins. Lotta always jumped on a horse if she could!

They came to the circus field. Everyone there was on the move. The tents were down. The cages were in order. The caravans were passing out of the big gate one by one, Jumbo pulling three of them as usual. There was a great deal of shouting and yelling. It was all most exciting.

Jimmy's father joined the line of caravans. Jimmy leaned out of his caravan. He saw Jumbo a good way in front, plodding along steadily—good old Jumbo. He saw Lilliput with Jemima the monkey cuddling him. He caught sight of Mr. Galliano shouting to someone, his hat well on one side.

Soon the field was empty. The circus was on the way to its next stopping-place. And with it were Jimmy and his mother and father, cosy in their caravan, wondering where they were going to, and what was going to happen to them.

"We've got a house on wheels, Mum," said Jimmy happily. "I've always wanted to live in one. We belong to the circus now. Oh, isn't it lovely?"

Jimmy's mother busied herself in putting up the bed. There was very little room left in the caravan when that was up! Jimmy had to sit on it when he looked out of the window—but usually he sat on the top step at the door, whistling a merry tune as the circus procession passed through villages and towns, enjoying all the stares and shouts he got. Ah—Jimmy felt very grand—for he was a proper circus-boy now!

THE CIRCUS GOES ON THE ROAD

The first day that Jimmy travelled with the circus was really very exciting. The circus had to go slowly, for Jumbo the elephant plodded along in a very leisurely manner, and the caravans kept up with him. Sometimes the horses went on a good way in front and left old Jumbo behind with the three caravans he pulled — but then the horses had a good rest later on, so that Jumbo always caught up with them in the end.

Anyway, nobody ever minded how slow or fast the procession went along. Mr. Galliano always decided how long they were to be on the road to the next town. He sent one of his men in front of him to paste up great posters in the town they were going to, telling the people there about the circus.

This time they were to be two days on the road. They were going to a very big town — the town of Bigchester — and it was a long way off. They hoped to be there on Tuesday night, and by Thursday evening everything would be ready for the circus to give its first show. Lotta told Jimmy all this as they went along. She had come to Jimmy's caravan and was sitting on the steps with him, being jolted up and down. Their caravan was being pulled by one of the ordinary horses, not one of the show horses, who were only used for pulling Mr. Galliano's carriage.

"Oh, Jimmy, I *am* so glad you are coming with us!" said Lotta, her blue eyes shining like forget-me-nots. "I shall have you to help me every day now. I wonder what jobs Mr. Galliano will give you to do. You'll help with the animals, I expect."

"Yes, that's what I'm to do," said Jimmy proudly. "But

I say, Lotta—won't it be funny not going to school? I've always been, you know—and now I shan't go any more."

"*I've* never been in my life," said Lotta. "I can read a tiny bit, but I can't write."

"Lotta!" said Jimmy, in horror. "You can't *write*! How dreadful!"

"It isn't dreadful," said Lotta, going red. "*I* don't mind! I've got nobody to write letters to, have I?"

"You want writing for other things besides that," said Jimmy. "*I* shall teach you to read and write properly, Lotta. You will have to come to our caravan in the evening, and I'll show you my books and teach you lots of things."

"All right," said Lotta. But she didn't look very pleased. Lotta didn't want books—they seemed dull to her. She made up her mind to be silly and stupid when Jimmy was trying to teach her, so that he would soon give it up.

Lilliput waved to them from the next caravan. He too was delighted that Jimmy was coming with them. Everyone liked the merry little boy.

"Hallo, Lilliput!" shouted Jimmy to the little fellow. "How are Jemima and the other monkeys? Were they frightened of the storm last night?"

"Not a bit!" yelled back Lilliput. "Jemima got down under the bedclothes and cuddled my feet. She always does that if there's a noise going on outside. The others never made a sound."

"Oh, fancy having a monkey cuddling your feet all night!" said Jimmy, surprised. That was the best of a circus. The most extraordinary and amusing things happened every day. Jimmy beamed. He was very happy. He could hear his mother in the caravan singing a little song. She was happy too. His father had a good job with the circus, Jimmy was going to work too, and she was going to be with them. Everything was lovely.

Just them the caravan went over a big stone and gave such a jolt that Jimmy fell off the steps and rolled on the ground. Lotta laughed till she cried. "That shows you're not a real circus-boy," she said. "A real circus-boy would never fall off caravan steps. Oh, you did look funny, Jimmy!"

Jimmy gave the cheeky little girl a push, and *she* rolled down the steps too. But almost before she reached the ground she turned a half-somersault, landed on her hands and swung over on to her feet again as lightly as a cat—and she was up on the caravan steps beside Jimmy giving him a hard pinch before he could say a word!

"Ow!" shouted Jimmy, for Lotta could give some really dreadful pinches. "Don't!"

"Now, now, you two," said his mother from inside the caravan. "Those steps are not a very safe place to quarrel on. Lotta, what *have* you done to your hair? It looks dreadful. Did you brush it this morning?"

"*Brush it!*" said Lotta, in surprise. "Of course not, Mrs. Brown. I only brush it when I'm going into the circus-ring when the show is on."

"Goodness gracious!" said Mrs. Brown. "No wonder it always looks so untidy. Now, Lotta, if you like to go and make yourself really clean and tidy, you can come and have a meal with us. I've got some sardines and a new ginger cake."

"Oooh!" said Lotta, who was nearly always hungry, just like Jimmy. "All right. I'll go and do what I can. It seems a waste of time, and Lal, my mother, will think it very queer when she sees me tidying up—but I'd love to have something to eat."

She jumped to the ground and ran off to her own caravan. Jimmy laughed.

"Oh, Mother!" he said. "I'm sure you'll never change Lotta. She always has dirty hands and untidy hair, and she doesn't care a bit if she has any buttons on or not."

"Well, Jimmy, don't you get it into your head that you're going to get like *that*," said his mother firmly. "Circus-folk are kindly, good people, but I do think they might be a bit cleaner and tidier; and Lotta's got to learn that I shall not let her come to meals here unless she sits down as clean and tidy as we do. Now, come here and wash your hands."

Jimmy squeezed into the caravan. Really, there was hardly room to move, with the bed and the stove and the tiny folding table. He dipped his hands into the bowl of water and washed them. He wetted his hair and brushed it. His mother was busy cutting up the ginger cake. It did look good!

Lotta soon came back. She looked quite different. Her hair shone and her face and hands were clean.

"Good girl, Lotta," said Jimmy's mother. Lotta was pleased, she liked Jimmy's mother.

"You must sit on the steps and eat your meal there," said Mrs. Brown. "There's no room in here. I'll give your father a sandwich and a piece of cake too, through this little front window."

Jimmy's father was driving the horse in front. They could hear him whistling as he sat there, enjoying the May sunshine and the sweet-smelling hedges as he passed them. Jimmy's mother pushed open one of the little windows that looked out to the front of the caravan. She put out her hand and tapped Mr. Brown on the shoulder. He turned round in surprise.

"Sandwiches and cake for you, Tom," said Mrs. Brown, and he took them in delight, for he too was very hungry. Soon everyone was eating hard, and there wasn't a scrap left of that ginger cake by the time Jimmy and Lotta had finished.

"Oh, I do think this is fun!" said Jimmy, looking up into

the blue sky. "Jogging along like this, nothing to worry about, no school tomorrow, holidays all the time."

"Holidays!" said Lotta in surprise. "Why, Jimmy, whatever are you talking about? The only holidays we circus-folk get are the days when we travel, like this! It's hard work all the rest of the time. Yes, and you just wait till we get to Bigchester and begin to unpack everything— you'll hear Mr. Galliano shouting at everyone then and, my word, you'll have to skip round and do your bit too. You don't know what hard work is yet. School is play compared to circus life."

The circus caravans, cages, and carriages jogged on through the long May day. The dogs yapped and barked in their cages, for they were hot and restless. Jimmy slipped along to see if they had plenty of water to drink. Such a lot of it got spilt during the jolting of the journey. He filled their big stone bowls up again, and gave them a handful of dry biscuits. They crowded round him, licking his hands and jumping up, delighted to see him. The sun shone down hotly into their big cage. Jimmy saw a blind rolled up at the top of the cage, and he pulled it down so that they might have shade. One little dog was bad-tempered with the heat and he was put into a separate cage, where he could lie quietly by himself. There were three or four of these separate cages at one end of the big caravan-cage, so that any dog could be separated from the others at times.

Usually they loved to be with one another, playing and rolling about, for they were a happy, healthy lot, very good-tempered and jolly. Jimmy peeped in at the little dog who was separated from the others and gave him some fresh water too. "Woof!" said the dog gratefully.

"We'll give them a run when we get to our camping-ground tonight," said Lotta. "It will be fun to go off for a walk this evening."

On and on went the circus caravans through the May evening. The sun was sinking now, but the days were long and full of light.

Jimmy thought Jumbo must be very hot plodding all day in the sun—but Jumbo didn't seem to mind much. Once Mr. Tonks stopped the caravan and took Jumbo to a stream nearby. Jumbo put his long trunk into the water and then lifted it up and squirted the cool water all over his dusty back. He did this a good many times till he was really cool, and then he suddenly squirted Jimmy and Lotta, who were standing watching him.

Lotta jumped out of the way in time, but Jimmy was soaked. How Lotta laughed!

"He often does that for a joke," she said. "I guessed he was going to do it. Oh, how wet you are, Jimmy!"

Jimmy laughed too, and Jumbo gave a loud snort. "Hrrumph!"

"He's laughing too," said Mr. Tonks, his keeper.

About eight o'clock, when the sun was low behind the trees and the shadows were very long indeed, Mr. Galliano called a halt. They had come to a shady piece of woodland, and there was a brook nearby for water.

At once everything was bustle and flurry. The horses were taken out of the line and allowed to graze. The caravans were turned on to the grass, and the steps of each were let right down to the ground. The dogs began to bark, for they knew that a walk was near at hand. Jemima the monkey left Lilliput and darted up a tree, where she sat chattering and laughing. The other monkeys, who were not so tame as Jemima, were safely in their big roomy cage.

Fires were made and soon delicious smells stole through the air. It was such a glorious evening that everyone ate in the open air. It was warm, and the scent of nearby hawthorn, which lay like a drift of snow over the hedges, came all round the camp, making everyone sniff in delight.

Jimmy's mother saw everybody making a fire near their caravans and she thought she would too. But she did not know the trick of making a camp-fire and soon she was quite in despair. Jimmy had gone off to help his father with some of the horses, and Mrs. Brown thought she would never be able to cook her herrings.

But Lotta came skipping along to help. "We'll get it all done by the time Jimmy and Brownie are back," she cried. "I'll do the fire for you, Mrs. Brown."

And by the time Jimmy and his father came back, the fire was crackling, the herrings were cooking, and it looked too lovely for words.

"Oh, I *am* going to enjoy my first evening camping out!" cried Jimmy.

THE FIRST NIGHT IN THE CARAVAN

Jimmy thought that herrings had never tasted so nice before! It was getting dark now and the fire they were sitting round glowed red and yellow. There were two herrings for everyone, and hot cocoa and bread and butter. Jimmy ate hungrily. Everyone chattered and laughed. It was nice to be at rest again after a day of jolting and jerking.

The circus horses grazed peacefully. They were tethered by long ropes, so they could move about freely. Someone had to keep awake and watch over them all night long, for they were valuable horses. Jumbo the elephant was having a good feast, for he was hungry too. They could hear him saying, "Hrrumph, Hrrumph!" now and again, as if he were talking to himself. Mr. Tonks had tethered him to a very big tree with a very strong wire-rope this time—for he did not want to lose Jumbo again if a storm came.

The light of several camp-fires shone out in the piece of open woodland. Mr. Galliano called one of his men to him and sent him round to each caravan.

"All fires to be out in half-an-hour's time," said the man. Lotta explained why.

"We never leave any fire burning at night," she said. "A scrap of burning paper blowing out in the wind might set a wooden caravan or cage on fire. So Galliano always sets a time for every fire to be out."

They sat around it for a little while longer, and then someone yelled for Lotta.

"Lotta! Where are you? What about those dogs? They are barking their heads off."

"Come on, Jimmy!" said Lotta, getting up. "We must take the dogs for their walk before it gets too late."

"Dear, dear!" said Mrs. Brown, who didn't like these late nights for Jimmy at all. "Must you really go, Jimmy? You ought to be in bed!"

"He can sleep in the day when we're travelling, if he's tired," said Mr. Brown. "Circus hours are different from those of ordinary folks, Mary. Go on, Jimmy—take the dogs with Lotta. I'll put out the fire."

The two children set off with the dogs. How pleased the animals were to stretch their legs! Lotta and Jimmy set free three of the dogs who were really obedient and would come when they were whistled—the others had to go on the big leads. They set off down a little lane that seemed to lead to a hillside.

"Isn't it lovely, Lotta!" said Jimmy, sniffing the white may as they passed it. "And look at the moon!"

The moon was coming slowly up over the hill in front of them. The countryside was bathed in light, pale and cold and silvery. Everything could be seen quite plainly, and Lotta and Jimmy thought it was just like daytime, but with the colours missing.

It was a lovely walk. The two children were tired but they were glad to stretch their legs, too, for they had been riding for many hours. The dogs pulled at their lead, and the three who were free tore up and down and round about as if they were quite mad.

They did not meet anyone, for the countryside just there was quite deserted. Only a lonely farmhouse shone in the moonlight not far off. A dog there barked loudly.

"Now it's time to go back," said Lotta. "My goodness, I'm sleepy! Come on, Punch! Come on, Judy! Where's Darky? Whistle him, Jimmy. Your whistle is louder than mine."

Jimmy whistled. Darky came rushing up, and they turned back. "I'm going to try and teach *all* the dogs to come as soon as they are whistled," said Jimmy. "Then we can let the whole lot off the lead whenever we like, Lotta, and they will be able to have a glorious run."

Back they went to the camp, singing loudly. Lotta knew old circus songs, and Jimmy knew songs he had learnt at school. First one sang, and then the other. It was fun. The dogs seemed to like it, for they were all quiet and good.

When they got back to the camp, all the fires were out and everyone was getting ready to go to bed. Lilliput and Jemima were already in their caravan, and Jimmy wondered if the little monkey was cuddling Lilliput's feet again, or was snuggled round his neck. He thought it must be funny to sleep with a little monkey cuddled up to you always!

"Jimmy! What a long time you've been!" called his mother, as the little boy helped Lotta to put the dogs into their big cage, and feed them. "Hurry now—it's time you were in bed."

"Good-night, Lotta," said Jimmy, as he heard Laddo, Lotta's father, calling her. "See you tomorrow!"

The two sped off to their different caravans. Jimmy's mother had a bowl of cold water from the brook nearby for him to wash in. In a trice he was in his pyjamas and was cuddling down on the little mattress on the floor of the caravan beside his parents' bed. What fun to sleep in a house on wheels!

"Good-night, Jimmy," said his mother, who was already in bed. "Shut the caravan door now, Tom. I know it's a hot night—but really, I can't do as the others do yet, and leave the door open."

So the door was shut and all the little windows were opened to let in the sweet air of the May night. Jimmy threw off one of his blankets. It really was too warm to have two! He lay there with one over him, listening to the call of an owl in the wood, and seeing a big white star through the side window. He heard one of the horses whinny and a dog whine.

"I'm one of the circus-folk now," he thought sleepily. "I'm one of the circus-f—f—f . . ."

And then he was fast asleep, dreaming of a long white road he had to follow with his caravan. He slept all night long without waking—and do you know, he didn't even wake when his mother slipped out of bed in the morning and opened the caravan door! She had to walk right over Jimmy, and she laughed when she saw him sleeping there so peacefully.

The sun was up, and the countryside was golden. The sky was a pure blue, and everything looked new and fresh. Jimmy's mother stood looking out. She was happy. This was different from being in a town, in a dirty little street, with a tiny backyard and not a tree to be seen.

When Jimmy woke up at last there was quite a bustle going on in the camp. Everyone was having breakfast, the horses had been watered. Jumbo had been fed, the dogs had been seen to, and there was a lovely smell of frying bacon and sausages.

Jimmy sat up. "Wherever am I?" he said to himself in astonishment, looking round the old caravan, which seemed dark compared with the bright sunshine outside. Then he remembered and gave a shout. "Hurrah! I'm with the circus! Mother! Where are you?"

"Out here, Jimmy, cooking breakfast!" cried his mother. "Go and wash in the brook. Your towel is on your blanket."

Jimmy put on his things and scampered down to the brook. Oooh! The water was cold! He ran back to the caravan as hungry as a hunter, brushed his hair, and squatted down on the grass to eat a piece of bacon and a brown sausage. Lotta was having breakfast with Lal and Laddo not far away, and she waved to him.

"Sleepy-head!" she shouted.

"Lotta peeped at you four times this morning to see if you were awake, but you weren't," said Mrs. Brown. "I wouldn't let her wake you. You're not used to circus hours yet, and I don't want you to get tired out at the beginning."

"Oh, Mother, I shan't!" said Jimmy. "Oh, I *am* sorry I didn't wake before. Are we going off early?"

"Yes, soon after breakfast," said his father. "I've got to go and help with the horses, so you must give your mother a hand, Jimmy."

He went off, and Jimmy washed up for his mother, and did what he could. She sent him to the farm to buy six new-laid eggs and a pint of milk. When Lilliput saw him going he went with him, Jemima sitting on his shoulder as usual.

"New-laid eggs!" said Lilliput, rattling his money in his pocket. "I'll buy some, too; and you'd like one, wouldn't you, Jemima darling?"

Jemima made a chattering noise and bit Lilliput's ear gently. Then she sat on the very top of his head, and when the farmer's wife came to the door and saw the monkey there, she fled away screaming down the passage.

"It's all right!" shouted Jimmy. "It's only a tame monkey! Please can we have some new-laid eggs and some milk. I've got a jug!"

The farmer's wife peeped round the corner of the passage. "You take that monkey away," she called to Lilliput. "Nasty fierce creature!"

Lilliput grinned and put Jemima under his arm. The farmer's wife fetched a dozen new-laid eggs and filled Jimmy's jug with milk. Then she shut the door very firmly.

Jimmy laughed and went back to the camp with Lilliput. The horses were all harnessed and ready to go. Jumbo was out in the road, flapping his big ears, with Mr. Tonks beside him. Mrs. Brown was standing at the door of her caravan waiting for Jimmy to come.

"Hurry, Jimmy!" she cried. "We are just off!"

All the fires were stamped out. Every bit of rubbish had been picked up and burned before the camp was ready to go. Mr. Galliano would never let any mess be left behind, for he said that made people think circus-folk were as rubbishy as their litter. And, my goodness! If anyone dared to leave papers or tins behind, what a temper Mr. Galliano flew into. He was a marvellous man, kind but firm, good-hearted but hot-tempered, and everyone loved him and tried to please him.

There came the loud crack of a whip, sounded three times—the signal to go. The horses started off, and Jumbo put his best foot forward. Lilliput jumped on his caravan and waved to Jimmy. Oona the acrobat was there, and Sticky Stanley the clown was sitting in his rather dirty caravan, singing a new and funny song he had made up the day before. The circus was on the move!

Down the road they went, some of the caravans sending up smoke from their stoves through the little chimneys. Mr. Galliano sat in state in his carriage, his top-hat on one side. Mrs. Galliano, fat and good-tempered, sat beside him. Nobody knew her very well. She kept herself to herself and waited on Mr. Galliano all day long. The lovely horses drew the carriage along in great style.

"Galliano's always in his carriage dressed like that when we drive through the towns near our show-place," said Lotta to Jimmy. "Everyone turns out to see him and that makes them talk about the circus and they come to see it. We'll get to Bigchester about tea-time, I expect."

Jimmy settled himself down for the day's travelling. It

was exciting to see everything they passed. The circus went through little villages and big towns, through the green countryside and by big and little farms. Everyone came out to watch the procession. Mr. Galliano bowed to left and right like a king, and the trumpeters on the horses in front blew loudly. "Tan-tan-tara! Tan-tan-tara!"

People stared at Jimmy as he passed, and he felt very proud. "I wonder what that boy does in the circus!" somebody said. "Perhaps he walks the tight-rope."

"No, he doesn't!" yelled back naughty little Lotta. "He just gives the elephant its bath and puts it into its cot at night!"

LOTTA GIVES JIMMY A
RIDING LESSON

At about five o'clock the circus came to its next camping-place, where it was to stay for three weeks. The circus-folk had been there before, some years back, and they said that the people of Bigchester were very generous and came often to see the circus, so that Mr. Galliano and everyone made a lot of money.

Jimmy was pleased to hear this. "We shall be able to buy some paint and paint the old caravan up a bit," he said to his father. "And I'd like some pretty curtains at the windows, like those Mr. Galliano has in his caravan."

But Mr. Brown had no time to talk when the circus reached its camping-place. The odd-job man in a circus has a hundred bits of work to do, all different, and many of them to be done all at once. Mr. Brown hurried here and there and everywhere, he was shouted for by everybody, most of all by Mr. Galliano, who seemed to be in twenty different places at once.

The caravans turned into a huge field. The cages were all set in one corner. The caravans were set in a wide circle together. The wagons and vans that held all the circus benches and tents and odds and ends were put in the middle. That was where the great circus-tent was to be put up. Brownie, as everyone called Jimmy's father, hurried to and fro, giving a hand here and a hand there.

Mr. Galliano shouted and yelled, and Jumbo the elephant lifted his trunk and trumpeted loudly as if he were trying to drown Galliano's big voice. Lotta laughed. She always kept out of the way when the circus was settling into camp, for she had found out that grown-ups were very cross when they were busy. She and Jimmy were underneath Jimmy's caravan, packing away things that need not be kept inside the small caravan—the wash-tub, a box of all kinds of things, a trunk of clothes, and an odd saucepan or two. Really, the caravan was so tiny that even a saucepan seemed in the way.

For four hours there was a bustle and noise and shouting. Then gradually it died down. The camp was settling in. The horses were the first animals to be looked after always, for they had to be kept simply perfect. They were now peacefully eating the grass at one end of the field, under the eye of George, one of the horsemen. Jumbo was tied up to a strong post—and how Jimmy laughed to see that the post was itself tied to the front of Mr. Tonks's caravan!

"Mr. Tonks, Mr. Tonks!" shouted the little boy, "if Jumbo runs away again in the middle of the night, he'll drag his post off and the post will drag off your caravan, and you'll go bumping all over the place!"

"Just what I planned," said Mr. Tonks, with a grin. "I'm not going to have Jumbo sneaking off by himself any more. No—if he goes, he takes me with him."

A great many people from the town had come to watch the circus settling in. Jimmy felt proud as he walked about, for he could see that the boys who were watching wished very much that they belonged to the circus too. Jimmy hoped that Lotta wouldn't tell them that he bathed the elephant at night and put it to bed, as she had told the people along the road. Really, you never knew what that little monkey of a Lotta was going to say!

"We begin the circus on Thursday night," said Mr. Galliano to his folk. "Everything must be ready then."

That night Jimmy lay on his little mattress in the caravan again, and he slept so soundly that he didn't hear Jumbo trumpeting in the night because Jemima the monkey had felt too hot in her caravan and had slipped out and played a little trick on old Jumbo. She had crept up behind him as he lay sleeping in the field, and tickled one of his big ears with a stick she had found.

Jumbo flapped his ear and slept on. Jemima tickled his ear again. Jumbo flapped it once more. Jemima went on, and at last Jumbo woke up and trumpeted loudly when he saw the naughty little monkey sitting nearby. Mr. Tonks poked his head out of his caravan door and shouted to Jumbo to be quiet. Jemima slipped away, chattering to herself in glee. She could really be a very naughty little creature, though everyone loved her and never seemed to mind what she did.

The next day there was a great bustle again. Banging and hammering went on all day long. The great circus-tent was put up. It rose high into the air, and Jimmy helped to knock in the pegs that held the ropes for it. Then the benches were unpacked and carried to the tent. Three of them had to be mended, and Jimmy's father soon did that.

"Come with me into the circus-ring, Jimmy," said Lotta that afternoon, when the tent was up. "I've got to practise some more riding, Laddo says. He's got the horses ready. You come too and watch me."

Jimmy went with Lotta. She was not wearing her lovely fluffy circus-frock, but just her old jersey and skirt. She kicked off her shoes when she got into the great red ring. Laddo, her father, was there waiting, and so was Lal, her mother. They smiled at Jimmy.

"I'll have to teach you to ride too, Jimmy," said Laddo. "You won't be a real circus-boy till you can ride any horse under the sun."

Jimmy watched Laddo and Lal practising their marvellous riding. They had three white horses there and they rode them bareback, sitting frontways and backways and sideways, kneeling, standing, balancing on one leg and then on the other. It was wonderful to watch them.

"Now, Lotta!" said her father. "Come along! Do your tricks quickly, because we want you to learn a new one."

Lotta leapt lightly up on to the back of a horse. She rode round the ring once, and then jumped to her feet on the horse's back. Up and down, up and down on the horse's back she went as it galloped round the ring, standing there as lightly as a fairy.

Laddo took another horse and let it run side by side with Lotta's horse. "Jump on to his back now, Lotta!" he said. "Jump! Here is the place to jump—I have marked it in black."

Jimmy saw that the broad part of the horse's back was marked with a black ring. That was where Lotta was to jump. Jimmy felt afraid. He hoped she wouldn't fall.

"Will you catch her if she falls?" he asked Laddo anxiously.

"She won't be hurt if she does fall," said Laddo, laughing, and Lotta laughed too.

"Now, jump!" shouted Laddo, running with the second horse. Lotta jumped—and landed most beautifully on the other horse's back, just where Laddo had marked the black ring. She kept her balance for half a moment, then lost it —and slipped gracefully down on to the horse's back, laughing.

"No, that won't do, Lotta," said Laddo. "Try again. You must keep your balance, and then, when you have ridden round the ring once, jump back to your own horse again."

Lotta slithered down from the second horse and jumped lightly on to her own horse again. She stood up and waited her time. At exactly the right moment the little girl jumped and landed neatly on the second horse's back. She stood there, trying to get her balance, and this time she was quite all right. She gave a yell of delight and stood on one foot as she rode round, kicking the other in the air.

"Now back on the other horse, Lotta," shouted her father. So back she went, very lightly, but just missed her balance again and, to Jimmy's dismay, fell from the horse.

But he needn't have been frightened. Lotta was like a cat and always fell on her feet. She landed lightly on the red plush ring itself.

Laddo was cross with her and so was Lal, her mother. "I shall send Jimmy out if you don't work properly," scolded Lal. "You will spend the rest of the evening practising, Lotta, and if you can't do it properly then, you will get up at five o'clock tomorrow morning and practise again."

Lotta sulked. She jumped on to her horse again and began practising properly. Whilst she was riding round and round, jumping to and fro, Sticky Stanley the clown came in.

"All right, Lotta; don't stop," he said. "I've come to practise some new somersaults. But I want to do them round the red plush ring itself, so you won't worry me."

The clown, who didn't look at all like a clown today, because he was dressed in a yellow jersey and a dirty pair of grey flannel trousers, began to turn somersaults round the red ring. Over and over he went, and only once fell off. He fell right under the feet of one of the horses, but the horse neatly jumped over him and went on again without losing a step.

"Hey, Jimmy, you come and do a few somersaults," said Stanley the clown. Lotta stopped the horses to give them a rest, and watched Sticky Stanley teaching poor Jimmy.

Jimmy could do one head-over heels quite well, but he couldn't possibly do about twelve, one after another, as Stanley could. It made him giddy to do even three.

"Jimmy, you said you couldn't ride," said Lotta. "Come along up on my horse and see if you can."

"But I'd fall off!" said Jimmy, in horror. "Your horse hasn't any saddle or stirrups."

"You must learn to ride bareback or you'll be no use on a horse," laughed Lotta. "Come on, up you get!"

And up Jimmy had to get. He held on to the reins for dear life, and thought that a horse was about the most slippery creature to sit on that he had ever met. He slithered first one way and then another, and at last he slid off altogether and landed with a bump on the ground.

Sticky Stanley and Lotta held on to one another and laughed till the tears ran down their faces. They thought it was the funniest sight in the world to see poor Jimmy slipping about on the solemn, cantering horse.

"Oh, Stanley, if you could only do that at the circus tomorrow night, the people would laugh till they cried," said Lotta.

"That's an idea, Lotta!" said the clown. He looked at Jimmy. "Get up on the horse's back and do that again, old chap," he said. "If I see it once more I'll be able to do it myself."

"No, thank you," said Jimmy firmly, rubbing himself hard where he had been bumped.

"Go on, Jimmy, be a sport," said Lotta.

So Jimmy changed his mind and got on Lotta's horse again. But it was just as bad as before, Jimmy simply could *not* stay on that horse. It bumped him up into the air, and then when he came down again the horse was just bumping up, and knocked his breath out of him, and he began to slide about, first this way and then the other, being bumped all the time. At last he slid right off the back of the horse over the tail, and came down with such a bump that he couldn't breathe for a minute.

Stanley and Lotta sat down on the ground and laughed again till their sides ached. "I must do that, I simply must," said the clown. He got up and went to Lotta's horse which galloped solemnly round and round the ring the whole time. Of course Stanley could ride very well indeed —but this time he pretended he was Jimmy, and slithered about and gave great groans and grunts, and at last fell right underneath the horse and got all tangled up with his own legs.

"Well, if I was as funny as that, no wonder you laughed at me," said Jimmy, who had laughed so much that he couldn't stand up. "Do that tomorrow night, Stanley."

"Right!" said Stanley. I will! I'll have your horse for that, Lotta. She's careful with her feet."

"It *will* be fun when the show opens again tomorrow!" said Jimmy. "I *am* looking forward to it!"

78

A GOOD TIME FOR THE CIRCUS

By the next night the circus was all ready. Everyone had worked hard all Wednesday and Thursday, and now, by six o'clock, everything was spick and span.

Lotta came to Jimmy's caravan and begged Mrs. Brown to iron out her fluffy skirt. "Lal, my mother, is so busy," she said. "Her frock has got torn and she is mending it."

So, Mrs. Brown heated her iron over the stove and ironed Lotta's pretty frock. It took a long time, and whilst it was being done, Lotta washed her hair and dried it.

"Can you do that jumping trick all right now, Lotta?" asked Jimmy anxiously.

"Of course!" said Lotta. "It's easy! You watch me tonight, Jimmy. I'll get more claps than anyone."

When the frock was finished, the little girl ran off happily. She loved the times when the show was on. She loved the glare of lights in the big tent, the smell of the warm horses, and the shouts and whip-cracks of Mr. Galliano when he went into the ring.

One by one the circus-folk slipped from their caravans and ran across to the big tent to get their animals or to find their things. Oona the acrobat placed his ladder ready and his tight-rope. Sticky Stanley blew up some big balloons he was going to be silly with that night. Lilliput took his monkeys with him, and Jimmy saw that Jemima had on a new pink skirt and little bonnet.

The townspeople streamed in at the gate. A man stood there blowing a trumpet—tan-tan-tara! It sounded exciting. "Come to the circus, tan-tan-tara! Come to the circus, tan-tan-tara!"

Jimmy too had been busy. Every one of the dogs had

been well brushed twice that day. They were all eager to get into the ring and do their tricks. They pawed at their cage-door and yapped to be out. They had been for a good long walk that day with Jimmy and Lotta, but they wanted to stretch their legs again. Jumbo the elephant flapped his big ears to and fro and trumpeted to the people round him. He too wanted to get into the lighted ring and show what he could do!

The circus began. Jimmy stood outside the entrance that the performers used, and got things ready for them. He held the horses until it was time for them to go into the ring. He handed Oona the acrobat his ladder, and got his tight-rope ready for him. He gave Lilliput the little table and chairs that his monkeys used when they had their tea-party in the middle of the ring. He was very useful indeed.

When Jumbo the elephant was plodding into the ring to play cricket with his keeper, Mr. Tonks, Jimmy saw Mr. Tonks making anxious signs to him.

"The ball—the ball, Jimmy!" said Mr. Tonks. He had put it down somewhere and couldn't find it. Jimmy guessed that Jemima the monkey had gone off with it, and he raced off to his own caravan. Underneath it was a box, and he knew that he had an old red ball of his own there. He found it, tore back to the tent and sent it rolling into the ring just in time. Mr. Tonks was pleased. Jimmy was really a most useful little boy!

After Jumbo had played cricket and had heaps of clapping and cheering, the three white horses went in, and Laddo, Lal, and Lotta rode them cleverly, standing on them, swinging from one to another and never falling once.

Jimmy watched for Lotta to do her new trick. She stood up on her own horse, a lovely little figure in a fairy-like frock, with long silver wings spreading behind her. She really did act like a fairy too, for she seemed to fly from one horse's back to another, she was so light.

Jimmy need not have worried about Lotta falling, for the little girl was as sure-footed as a goat. She jumped to and fro, always on the right spot, whilst the horses went solemnly galloping round and round the ring. People stood up in their seats and shouted loudly, for they thought Lotta was wonderful. Jimmy clapped too, from where he stood, peeping in at the entrance to the ring. How he wished he could do things like Lotta! But maybe he would be able to some day, if he practised hard.

Then in went Sticky Stanley the clown again to do his new funny trick on the horse. Jimmy watched him—he ran into the ring and jumped on to the back of Lotta's horse, which was still going round and round. The other two horses were led out by Lotta.

"Yoicks!" shouted the clown, pretending to gallop the horse—and then he began to slip off, just as Jimmy had done. First he went this way and got right again, and then he slid the other way, being bumped, bumped, bumped by the horse all the time! Oh dear, how everyone laughed! Then the clown hung round the horse's neck—then he slid back again—and at last slithered right off over the horse's tail, and landed with a bump on the ground, just as Jimmy did the day before!

Everyone laughed and shouted, and Sticky Stanley got even more clapping than he usually did. He was pleased when he ran out of the ring, doing somersaults every now and again.

He saw Jimmy standing by the ring-entrance and he grinned at him. "Hallo, youngster!" he said. "Your trick went well—didn't it?—but my word, I shall have a big bruise tonight. Here's something for you—catch!"

He threw something round and shining to Jimmy. The little boy caught it. It was a fifty new pence piece. Jimmy stared in delight. He had never had so much money in his life before!

The show went off very well indeed. Mr. Galliano was pleased. He wore his hat well over his right ear the next day, and Mrs. Galliano bought tins of fruit-salad for everyone and the biggest jug of cream that Jimmy had ever seen. It was fun eating fruit-salad and cream in the field for dinner next day. You never knew what was going to happen in a circus!

Jimmy was busy all that week. He helped with the dogs, and soon Lal and Laddo left them entirely to the two children, for they loved the dogs and could be trusted to look after them well. Jimmy helped Mr. Tonks with the elephant too, and learnt how to rub down the horses with George, one of the grooms. All the animals were good with Jimmy. It was really marvellous to see what he could do with them. When Darky got a bone in his throat and was in such pain that not even Mr. Galliano liked to go near him, Jimmy didn't mind.

He went up to poor Darky, who was almost choking, and put his hand right down Darky's throat. He felt the bone there, gave it a sharp twist, and up it came! Darky was so grateful that he licked Jimmy's shoes till they shone.

"Good boy, Jimmy, good boy—yes?" said Mr. Galliano. "You were not afraid of being bitten—no?"

"No, sir," said Jimmy. "Darky wouldn't bite me."

The circus-show went on until Saturday and began again on Monday. It did very well indeed, and Mr. Galliano always wore his hat well on one side. He gave Mr. Brown, Jimmy's father, an extra sum of money because he worked so hard and was so useful. Mr. Brown ran back to his caravan with it.

"Look!" he said to Jimmy and Jimmy's mother. "Two pounds! What about doing up the old caravan and making

82

it look nice?" Jimmy wanted to start painting at once.

So off went Jimmy and his father that afternoon to buy a tin of green paint and a tin of yellow paint. They meant to make their caravan really nice now. Jimmy's father mended one of the wheels which was really almost falling off, and he put the chimney on properly so that the smoke would not pour into the caravan but go streaming away outside.

In their spare time the two of them cleaned and painted the old caravan. You should have seen it! Jimmy's mother was really pleased. "I do hope you will have some paint left over for the inside," she said. "It is so dark here—I can often hardly see what I'm doing. For one thing the glass

83

in the windows is bad glass, and for another the smoke from the stove has made the walls very sooty."

"Soon alter all that," said Mr. Brown. "You just wait, Mary!"

By the end of the second week you wouldn't have known Jimmy's caravan. It was painted a nice bright green outside, and the wheels were green too, but the spokes were yellow. The window-sills were yellow and so was the chimney. Jimmy's father had enough money left to buy some cream-coloured paint for the inside of the caravan.

He painted it carefully, first putting all the furniture outside on the grass. "You'll have to finish before night, Dad," said Jimmy, "or we'll all have to sleep in the open air."

The inside of the caravan was very different when it was finished — so light and airy, and it looked twice as big! Jimmy's father put new glass into the windows too, and Jimmy slipped off to the town and bought some green and yellow fabric for curtains. He spent the money that the clown had given him.

"Lotta, will you make me these curtains for Mother?" he asked the little girl, giving her the parcel, as she sat eating a cake on the steps of her caravan.

"Make curtains!" said Lotta in surprise, and she laughed loudly. "You must be mad, Jimmy! I can't sew."

"Can't you *really* sew?" said Jimmy. "I thought all girls could. You aren't very clever at some things, Lotta. You can't write, you can't read properly, and you can't sew!"

"And *you* can't fall off caravan steps without getting bumped!" cried Lotta crossly, and she pushed Jimmy off so quickly that he slipped to the ground with a bang.

Jimmy marched off without a word. He went to his mother and gave her the parcel. "Mother, here's a present for you," he said. "I wanted Lotta to make the fabric into curtains for the caravan, but she can't sew."

His mother opened the parcel and cried out in delight. "Oh, Jimmy! How pretty it is—just the right colours to match the new paint on the caravan! You are a very kind little boy! Never mind about Lotta not being able to make them. I shall soon be able to make them—they won't take me more than an hour or two. And as for Lotta, I think she ought to learn a few things. I am going to teach her to read and write and sew—and in return perhaps Lal and Laddo will teach you to ride properly."

"Oh, Mother! That's a splendid idea!" said Jimmy, pleased. "I'll go and tell Lotta. Shall I do lessons with you too?"

"Of course," said his mother. "I'm not going to let you forget all you've learnt, Jimmy—and I can teach you a great deal that you ought to know."

"I'll go and find Lotta," said Jimmy, and off he went. But Lotta wasn't at all pleased.

"What? Do lessons!" she said, making a face. "I've never done any and I'm not going to begin now."

"But my mother wants to teach you, Lotta," said Jimmy. "I shall have to do some too."

"You can do them by yourself," said Lotta. "I won't come!"

"Oh yes, you will, Lotta!" said a voice behind her, and Laddo popped his head out of the caravan door. "It's quite time you learnt about a few things besides horses and dogs. I'll teach Jimmy all I know about horses and riding, and Jimmy's mother can teach you sewing and reading and sums and things that a little girl ought to know."

Lotta made a face and slipped down the steps. What a naughty little girl she could be when she wanted to! "Can't catch *me*, can't catch *me*!" she yelled to Jimmy—and off she flew over the field in a trice. It wasn't a bit of good going after her—Jimmy could never catch her!

POOR OLD PUNCH

The circus-show went on, night after night. Jumbo played cricket and got clapped and cheered. Jemima the monkey played her tricks in the ring, and the other monkeys sat down at their little table and had their meal, with hundreds of people watching them each night. The ten little terrier dogs, neat, smart, and happy, ran round the ring merrily, and Judy jumped through her hoops without once making a mistake. The circus-folk were happy.

Jimmy was happy too. He was busy all day long, for there was always something to do, and the little boy was willing to give a hand to everyone. Sometimes he was with Oona the acrobat and sometimes with Lilliput, watching him pet his monkeys. Every day he had a chat with old Jumbo the elephant, and, next to Mr. Tonks his keeper, Jumbo loved Jimmy, who often brought him tit-bits.

Oona gave Jimmy a pair of his old soft shoes, and taught him to walk the tight-rope. Once Jimmy had learnt to balance himself, he found this was quite easy.

Oona fastened the tight-rope only about a foot above the ground for Jimmy, so that he would not be frightened of falling. He gave the little boy a long pole to hold in his hands, for he said that would help him to get his balance well. Jimmy stepped on the rope — and at once fell off the other side.

Lotta came to watch. She laughed loudly, and Jimmy poked her with his pole.

"Go away!" he said. "I shall never learn anything if you watch me and laugh."

"Don't take any notice of Lotta," said Oona. "She needs a good spanking sometimes. You needn't laugh at Jimmy, Lotta—I've tried to teach *you* to walk the tight-rope before now, and you've fallen off each time. If you stand there laughing any more I'll put you on the rope and let Jimmy see you fall off. Then he can laugh at *you*."

Oona could be quite cross at times, so Lotta stopped giggling and watched Jimmy. She was rather surprised that the little boy learnt so quickly, for she had found it too difficult herself. Before the end of the morning Jimmy could walk the whole length of the tight-rope without falling off—though he wobbled like a jelly, Oona said.

"We'll call you the Tight-rope Jelly-walker," Oona said, with a grin. "Hundreds of people will come to see you."

Jimmy jumped off the rope and put on his own boots. "Thanks very much, Oona," he said. "I liked that. I'm learning to ride too. Stanley the clown thought I was so funny the first time I tried to ride, that he copied me in his turn at night, and that's why he got so much clapping this week."

"I know," said Oona, turning himself upside down and running about lightly on his two strong hands. "Come on, Jimmy—what about doing a little of this?"

"I want Jimmy now," said Lotta. "We've got to take the dogs out."

They went to the big cage. The dogs were lying quietly, some of them with their tongues out, for the weather was warm. One of them, Punch, did not get up and wag his tail when he saw Jimmy coming, as he usually did. Jimmy noticed it at once.

"Hallo! What's the matter with Punch?" he said. "He doesn't seem well."

He went into the cage and lifted up the dog's head. Punch wagged his tail feebly. His eyes were not bright, like the others, and he looked very miserable.

"Punch is ill," said Jimmy in alarm. "Oh, Lotta — what can be the matter with him?"

"I don't know," said Lotta. "Let's tell Lal."

They ran off to tell Lotta's mother, and she came running to see Punch. She was alarmed, for she thought perhaps all the dogs might catch the illness and then they would not be able to perform at night.

"I'll fetch Mr. Galliano," she said to Jimmy. "He knows more about animals than anyone in the world."

Very soon Mr. Galliano came along, his top-hat standing straight up on his head, for he was upset at the thought of one of the circus-animals being ill.

"Get Punch out of the big cage," he said to Jimmy. "He must be kept away from the other dogs."

Jimmy lifted Punch out of the cage. The dog licked the little boy's hand feebly.

Mr. Galliano took him gently on his knee and ran his hand over him. He looked at his eyes and his tongue and then he shook his head.

"Poor little dog — he'll be very ill," he said. "He's got an illness that will turn him yellow and make him very sick."

"Will he get better?" asked Lotta anxiously. "He is one of Lal's best dogs."

"I don't think he will get better," said Mr. Galliano, his gentle hands stroking the ill dog. "All you can do is to keep him warm and give him some medicine I'll let you have. Go and ask your father to make Punch a little kennel for himself, Jimmy."

Jimmy sped off. He was sad. He loved all the dogs and he didn't like to think that Punch was so ill. How could he have got ill? He was cared for so well! He must have met another dog when he was out and taken the illness from him.

"I shall nurse Punch myself," thought the little boy. "I *will* make him better! I will!"

Soon Brownie, Jimmy's father, was making a little kennel for Punch, who was now lying on a rug underneath Jimmy's caravan, not even the tiniest wag left in his tail.

"I'll nurse Punch," said Lotta to Jimmy. "He's my dog."

"No," said Jimmy. "I'm better with animals than you are, Lotta—you've often said so. I want to make Punch well again. Please let me."

"You can't," said Lotta. "Galliano says no dog gets better when he goes yellow like that. Look at his tongue, Jimmy—even that's gone yellow—and his eyes too. Poor Punch—he's such a darling."

"Did you get that medicine that Mr. Galliano said he had?" asked Jimmy.

Lotta pointed to a bottle on the grass. "He's to have it three times a day," she said.

"I shall feed him well too," said Jimmy.

"That's no use," said Lotta. "He won't want anything to eat, and if he does eat anything he'll be sick."

"Oh, Lotta, be quiet!" said Jimmy fiercely. "That's not helping me — telling me horrid things like that."

But Lotta was quite right. Poor Punch would not eat anything, and if Jimmy did manage to get something down his throat, the poor little dog was sick. It was dreadful.

Jimmy thought of nothing but Punch all that day and night and the next day. He could not think of anything to make the dog better. He was so feeble that he could hardly get out of his kennel. Jimmy slept beside him during the night.

Oona the acrobat came to see where Jimmy was on the third day, for the little boy had not gone to him for his daily practice on the tight-rope. When he saw Jimmy holding Punch's head on his lap, sitting beside his caravan, he understood.

"What's the matter with the old fellow?" he asked. "Oh, he's turned yellow, has he — that's the jaundice. I've never heard of but one dog getting better of that."

"Tell me," said Jimmy eagerly.

"Well, I once travelled with another circus," said Oona. "And they had three French poodles — you know, those dogs that have their fur clipped in such a funny way that parts of their body are bare. Well, one of them got yellow like this dog."

"Yes — go on," said Jimmy impatiently.

"Well, everyone said the dog would never get better," said Oona. "But there was an old woman in the circus, mother of one of the clowns there, and she cured him!"

90

"How?" cried Jimmy. "Tell me how!"

"I don't really know," said Oona. "She knew a lot about herbs and roots and plants, and she used to go out early in the morning and pick those she wanted. Then she would boil them and mix them, and make wonderful medicines. It was one of her own medicines she gave the dog."

"Do you remember what it was made of?" asked Jimmy.

"Of course not," said Oona. "That was years ago."

Jimmy almost cried with disappointment. "Oh, if only that old woman was in *our* circus!" he said.

"I know whose circus she's with," said Oona unexpectedly.

"*Do* you?" cried Jimmy. "Well—write to her then, Oona and ask her what we must give Punch. If we post the letter today, she'll get it tomorrow and we'll hear the next day —and that may be in time to save poor Punch."

"I can't write to her," said Oona. "I don't know how to write. I've never learnt."

"Good gracious!" said Jimmy. "Mother will have to teach you as well as Lotta. Never mind, Oona—tell *me* what circus the old woman is with, and *I'll* write."

"I don't know where the circus is," said Oona. "She's with Mr. Bang's circus, that's all I know."

Jimmy sighed in despair. He saw Mr. Galliano passing nearby and he got up and ran boldly to him.

"Mr. Galliano, sir," he said, "please could you tell me something? Do you know where Mr. Bang's circus is now?"

"Yes, at Blackpool," said Mr. Galliano, rather astonished. Jimmy shouted for joy and rushed back to Oona. "It's at Blackpool!" he said. "Now I'll write straight away. Mother! Mother! Have you got a piece of paper and an envelope?"

It took ages to find paper and envelope, but at last some was found, and Jimmy took a pencil and began to write.

"DEAR MRS. BENNITO [said Oona, and Jimmy wrote that down]. This is Oona the acrobat writing to you. Please send at once to tell us what medicine to give a dog who has gone yellow like that French poodle. Hope you are well. — OONA."

"I haven't any money for a stamp," said Jimmy. Oona gave him three pence and the little boy ran off to the town to buy the stamp and post the letter. How he hoped it would get to Mrs. Bennito quickly!

Jimmy went back to Punch, who was very weak, for as he wanted nothing to eat, he was going very thin indeed. Lotta was with him, crying. She had brought Punch some of her best chocolates — but of course the dog would not even sniff at them. Jimmy told her about the letter.

"Shall we have an answer today?" said Lotta, who had never had a letter in her life, and had no idea how long it took for letters to go and come.

"No," said Jimmy. "We can't have one till the day after next."

"That will be too late," said Lotta. "Oh, darling Punch, if only you would eat something!"

Now it so happened that Blackpool was not very far from Bigchester, and Mrs. Bennito got the letter that afternoon. She sent an answer at once — and the postman came with it to Mr. Galliano's circus the next morning. He gave the letter to Mr. Galliano, who sent it to Oona. It was a surprising thing for anyone in the circus to have a letter, except Mr. Galliano himself.

Oona rushed to Jimmy with the letter. "It's come — it's come!" he cried. "Read it, Jimmy. I can't!"

THE STRANGE MEDICINE

When Jimmy heard that the letter had come a whole day sooner than he expected, he was full of joy. He left Punch, whom he was nursing, and ran to Oona. He took the letter from him. Oona could not read, but Jimmy could.

Jimmy slit open the rather dirty envelope. The writing inside was small and difficult to read.

" 'Dear Oona' " he read — " 'This is what you must give the dog. Go and and get these things — one root of deadly nightshade — one root of — of — of ——' " Oh, I don't know what this is at all," said Jimmy in dismay. "Oona, the letter is full of the names of queer plants I don't know. It's no good!"

The little boy was so disappointed that he burst into tears. He had been up all night with Punch, and was tired out. Oona put his arm across his shoulders and patted him. "Now, now!" he said. "Don't upset yourself so. Take the letter to Galliano. He may be able to help you. He is a wonderful man."

Jimmy rubbed his tears away and ran to Mr. Galliano's caravan. The door was shut. Jimmy rapped on it.

"Who's there?" yelled Mr. Galliano. "Go away!"

"Oh, please, Mr. Galliano!" shouted Jimmy in despair. "Please, I want your help. It's for Punch."

Galliano opened the door. He was in a brilliant red dressing-gown with yellow braid. He looked quite strange without his top-hat. Mrs. Galliano, in an even brighter dressing-gown, was boiling a kettle on her stove.

Jimmy told Mr. Galliano about the letter and showed it to him. Mr. Galliano read it and whistled.

"Whew!" he said. "This needs a bit of understanding.

Here, Tessa—what do you make of it? You used to be good at this sort of thing—yes?"

Mrs. Galliano took the letter and read it through slowly, saying every word under her breath. Then she turned and looked at Jimmy, her kind eyes shining brightly.

"I know what all these things are," she said in her soft slow voice. "I knew Mrs. Bennito long ago. She is a marvellous old woman."

"Mrs. Galliano, how can I get those things, please?" said Jimmy. "Do you think they may cure poor old Punch? He is so thin and ill this morning."

"I will come with you to the woods and find these things," said Mrs. Galliano. "My mother was a gypsy and she knew of the magic powers there are in some roots and in many leaves and flowers. Go and tell your mother I will take you myself, and we will be back in three hours."

Jimmy ran off. His mother gave him a basket and put into it some sandwiches and a piece of chocolate cake, for Jimmy had not had any breakfast. He patted Punch and went to wait for Mrs. Galliano.

Lotta joined him. He told her what had happened. Her eyes opened wide.

"Oooh!" she said. "Fancy Mrs. Galliano going with you herself! She used to be marvellous, my mother said. She used to be the cleverest acrobat in the world, but then she got fat and gave it up. People were a bit afraid of her because her mother was a very clever gypsy, and I've heard it said that Mrs. Galliano would have been a witch in the old days."

Jimmy laughed. "What silly things you believe, Lotta!" he said. "Mrs. Galliano is no witch—I think she's kind and clever. Here she comes."

The caravan door opened and down the steps came Mrs. Galliano, dressed in a red skirt, a black blouse, and a yellow shawl, which was wrapped round her head. The caravan steps creaked, for Mrs. Galliano was indeed very big. She smiled her slow smile at Jimmy.

"Come!" she said. "We must hurry."

But there wasn't much hurrying, for Mrs. Galliano did not walk at all fast. She seemed to know the way to the woods without asking. She stopped once by a ditch and picked a plant which smelt horrible to Jimmy. He put it into his basket.

"Flower of woodruff," she said, "flower of woodruff. That is hard to find, for it is shy and small. Look for honeysuckle too, Jimmy. I need a root of that as well."

Jimmy hunted for honeysuckle, and Mrs. Galliano poked about looking for many other things. After some while the basket was empty of food and full of roots, leaves, and flowers. Mrs. Galliano read the letter for the last time. "I have everything now," she said. "There is one thing missing which cannot be found here—but I have found another plant that will do as well. We will go home, Jimmy."

Jimmy went back to the circus, carrying the basket. Mrs. Galliano took it from him and went up the steps of her caravan. "I know what to do with all these things," she said. "The medicine will be ready in two hours' time."

Jimmy never knew what Mrs. Galliano did with the strange roots and flowers she had gathered. He heard her pounding the roots, and Lotta said that she was boiling some of the plants in a big bowl, for she had seen them. Anyway, in about two hours' time Mrs. Galliano sent Lotta for Jimmy and gave him a bottle full of warm greeny-brown liquid.

"Give the dog two spoonfuls of this every half-hour," she said. "You know how to put it in at the side of his mouth, don't you?"

"Oh yes," said Jimmy, and he took the bottle eagerly.

95

He went to Punch. Poor Punch—he could not even lift his head now!

Jimmy lifted up the dog's nose and put back the loose skin at one side of the mouth. There was a gap between the teeth there, and anything could be neatly and quickly poured into the dog's mouth and so down the throat. Lotta held the bottle ready and Jimmy took the filled spoon from the little girl and tipped it gently into the dog's mouth, at the side. He held Punch's head up and the liquid flowed down his throat. Jimmy gave him another spoonful.

"I hope he won't be sick and waste it all," said Jimmy. "Good dog, Punch. Good dog."

The two children watched by the ill dog for half an hour and then gave him two more spoonfuls of the queer mixture. There did not seem to be any change in him.

"Let him be by himself for a while," said Jimmy's mother. "You can't do him any good by being with him just now. Run off and play for a little, or go and practise your riding, Jimmy."

Jimmy went off obediently, and practised riding with Lotta. He was much better on horseback now and had learnt to grip with his knees, so that he did not slip and slide about. Lotta was quite pleased with him, though she said he would never be a marvel.

They ran back to Punch at the end of the practise— and Jimmy gave a shout of joy.

"Lotta! He's wagging the end of his tail just a tiny bit! He must feel better! Where's the medicine?"

They gave the dog two more spoonfuls of it, and he actually lifted his head up himself to take it. He tried to lick Jimmy's hand but his tongue wouldn't come out far enough. Poor old Punch—he had indeed been ill!

Bit by bit that day the dog got better. He still would not eat anything, but when Mr. Galliano came over to

see him that night, he nodded his head.

"He is better — yes?" he said. "He is the first dog I have known who got over this illness — and it is all because of you Jimmy — yes? Tessa! Tessa! Come here!"

Mrs. Galliano came over to where Punch lay in his new kennel. She stroked him softly.

"It is wonderful medicine," she said. "Only Mrs. Bennito would know a thing like that. Here is her letter, Jimmy. Keep it safely, for you have there a cure for one of the worst illnesses animals have. He will get better now. I will send you a jar of food for him, and if you feed him with it tonight he will be much better tomorrow."

Lotta fetched the little jar of food. She read the label

on it. "Chicken essence," she said. "It sounds good, Jimmy! I should think Punch will like this."

Punch did. He licked the spoonful they gave him, and during that night he ate all that was in the jar. Gradually the yellow colour went from his eyes and tongue and skin, and he wagged his tail and gave a little yelp.

"He's better, he's better!" said Jimmy, beside himself for joy. "Oh, Lotta! I feel so happy!"

Lal and Laddo came to see Punch. Lal had been very unhappy about him, for she had had him since he was a puppy and had trained him herself. She was very clever with animals, but not so good with them as Jimmy when they were ill. She was very grateful to the little boy.

"The next time I hear of a good little pup I will buy him for you," she said to Jimmy. "It is a shame that a boy like you should have no dog of his own. Thank you, Jimmy, for being so good to Punch. He would have died if it hadn't been for you."

By the end of the week Punch was back in the show again, almost as frisky as ever! He simply adored Jimmy, and rolled over on his back in delight whenever the little boy came near. Mr. Galliano was proud of Jimmy too, for he said nobody else would have bothered to take all the trouble that Jimmy had taken to find out the medicine which had cured Punch.

The next exciting thing that happened was the coming of Sammy the chimpanzee. Mr. Galliano had been trying to hear of some other clever animal for his circus, and one day in walked Mr. Wally and his tame chimpanzee!

Jimmy was getting used to the queer folk and ways of the circus, but he *was* surprised to see the big chimpanzee walking along through the circus field, hand in hand with its master, Mr. Wally!

The chimpanzee was dressed in red trousers, blue coat, and straw hat, and it was smoking a cigarette! Jimmy stared in amazement. This was a wonderful sight.

"Good afternoon to you!" said Mr. Wally, taking off his own straw hat and bowing to the ground. "Have I the honour to be speaking to the great Mr. Galliano himself?"

Jimmy knew this was a joke, so he grinned and said, "No, and you jolly well know it! That's his caravan over there. I say! What a marvellous chimpanzee!"

"Ah, you don't know how marvellous he is!" said Mr. Wally, who was a big man with a remarkably small head. "He can ride a bicycle—he can undress himself and go to bed—he can get up in the morning and dress himself. But he won't clean his teeth."

By this time a little crowd had gathered around Mr. Wally and the chimpanzee. Mr. Galliano stuck his head out of his caravan and roared loudly.

"Hie! You want to see me—yes? Then come this way, and tell your chimpanzee to wipe his feet!"

Mr. Wally and the chimpanzee went up the caravan steps. "Oh," said Jimmy, "I do hope Mr. Galliano takes them for the circus. It *would* be fun to know a chimpanzee like that!"

"I shan't know the difference between you and the chimpanzee," said cheeky little Lotta, grinning at Jimmy. "You're so alike!" And then she sped away as Jimmy tore after her in a rage.

MR. WALLY'S WONDERFUL CHIMPANZEE

When Mr. Wally came down the steps again he was smiling broadly. Mr. Galliano had said he would take him and his chimpanzee into the circus. He was to go straight to the ring and show Mr. Galliano what he could do.

"Come on, Jimmy," said Lotta, appearing round a corner of the caravan. "Let's go and watch."

All the circus-folk went to the big tent and sat down on benches there to watch Mr. Wally and his chimpanzee. Mr. Wally appeared after a time, wheeling a big hand-barrow on which were a great many things covered up. These belonged to him and his chimpanzee, Sammy.

Sammy grinned at everyone and waved his hand to them. He was a young chimpanzee, high-spirited and happy, and he would do anything in the world for Mr. Wally, who had had him since he was a tiny baby. Sammy had been brought up just like a child. He had had a cot of his own, he had had his own clothes, and he had even been taught to count up to five!

Mr. Wally uncovered the things on his hand-barrow, and Jimmy saw that there was a cot there, taken to pieces, a little chair and folding table, and many other things. Mr. Wally quickly put up the cot, and placed a mattress, pillow, and blankets in it. He set up the table with a little mirror on it, and a brush and comb, a tooth-glass and a tooth-brush. He put a bowl of water on it, some soap, and a sponge.

"Surely the chimpanzee isn't going to use all those!" Jimmy said to Lotta.

She nodded. "I expect he will," she said. "Chimps are

very clever, you know, Jimmy. I saw one once before and he could write with a pencil. You can teach them a lot for a year or two, and after that they can't learn any more. They love learning, though—not like me!"

"Mr. Wally's ready now," said Jimmy. "Look! I say—the chimpanzee's undressing himself!"

So he was! At a sign from his master he took off his coat, folded it neatly and laid it on the chair. He slipped off his trousers and put them on the coat. He almost forgot to take off his straw hat, but remembered it in time. On the cot was laid a pair of red pyjamas. Sammy pulled on the trousers and put on the coat.

"He's put the coat on the wrong way round!" said Lotta, giggling.

The chimpanzee heard Lotta giggle, and he waved to her. He looked down at his coat, found that he couldn't button it, and took it off again to put it the right way round. Really, it was wonderful to see him, he seemed so sensible.

He got into his cot. He covered himself up—and then he pretended to snore. That made Jimmy laugh. Mr. Galliano laughed too.

"That is a new trick—yes?" he called to Mr. Wally. "I have not heard of that one."

"Taught him that last week," said Mr. Wally proudly. "Come on now, Sammy—time to get up!"

Sammy sat up in bed and yawned.

Lotta and Jimmy laughed in delight. What a wonderful chimpanzee! Sammy jumped out of bed and went to the little table. He took up his sponge and dipped it into the water. He sponged his face well and then, looking round for Mr. Wally, he threw the sponge straight at him, full of water!

It hit Mr. Wally on the nose and he gasped and spluttered. Jimmy laughed till he cried.

"Now, now, Sammy!" said Mr. Wally, putting the sponge back on the table. "That's quite enough!"

Mr. Galliano was pleased with that bit. He cocked his hat right on one side and beamed. The clever chimpanzee would be a great success in his circus.

"Get on, Sammy, get on," said Mr. Wally, seeing that Sammy was thinking of throwing the sponge at him again. Sammy took up his towel and dried himself. He even dried his feet, which he hadn't washed. That made Jimmy and Lotta laugh again.

Then he brushed his head neatly and combed it. He got up and brushed himself down with the hairbrush too. Then he began to unbutton his pyjama jacket.

"Clean your teeth, Sammy, clean your teeth," said Mr. Wally.

But that was just what Sammy wouldn't do. Although Mr. Wally had tried to teach him that trick for weeks on end, the chimpanzee would never do it properly. Do you know what he did? As soon as he put the tooth-brush into his mouth he bit all the bristles off! It was very expensive for Mr. Wally, who had to buy a dozen brushes at a time.

Sammy bit the bristles of the brush this time too and chewed them up, though Mr. Wally told him not to. Then he took off his pyjamas and dressed himself. He put on his straw hat.

"Now go to school, Sammy," said Mr. Wally. Sammy looked round and saw his satchel lying nearby. He picked it up and put it over his shoulder. He went to where a little bicycle was standing, hopped on it and rode round and round the ring, waving his hand, smiling broadly, and making funny barking noises.

"School-time!" said Mr. Wally, ringing a bell. Sammy hopped off his bicycle, took off his hat, and went and sat down on a chair.

In front of him Mr. Wally put some big numbers, drawn in black on white cards.

"Now you are at school, Sammy," he said. "Show me number three."

Sammy picked up the figure 3 and showed it to Mr. Wally and to everyone else. Jimmy and Lotta clapped loudly. They thought that was very clever.

"Now four," said Mr. Wally. And no matter what number his master said, the chimpanzee could pick it up. But as he could not count more than five, there were only five numbers there.

"Now tell me what one and two are," said Mr. Wally. The chimpanzee picked up the figure 3! Everyone clapped then, and Mr. Galliano went into the ring.

"Fine!" he said. "You can start tonight, Wally. Have you a cage for Sammy?"

"Yes," said Mr. Wally, pleased. "But at night he sleeps in my caravan with me. He has a cot there. I have brought him up just like a child."

"Won't it be fun to have a chimpanzee in the circus!" said Jimmy to Lotta, as they slipped out of the tent together to go and take the dogs for a walk. "I hope Mr. Wally will let me help him sometimes. You know, Lotta, I'd love to teach that chimpanzee to clean his teeth!"

"Pooh! You couldn't do that if Mr. Wally can't!" said Lotta. But Jimmy thought he could. He went to make friends with the chimpanzee that afternoon. He was sitting in a big cage behind Wally's yellow caravan, which had come along that afternoon to join the circus. Wally was well-off. He had a little car of his own, which pulled his caravan. Sometimes he unhitched the car from the caravan, put Sammy into the seat beside him, and went for a drive. Then how everyone stared to see Sammy sitting in his straw hat beside the driver!

"Can I go and talk to Sammy?" Jimmy asked. Mr.

Wally was polishing his car. He took a look at Jimmy.

"Are you the boy that went after that elephant some weeks ago and fetched him?" he asked.

"Yes," said Jimmy.

"Right," said Mr. Wally. "You can go and talk to Sammy all you like. He'll love you!"

So Jimmy unbolted Sammy's cage and went in to talk to him. The chimpanzee was sitting in a corner, pulling a newspaper to bits. He loved doing that. He looked up when Jimmy came in and stared at him. He made a chattering noise.

Jimmy went over to him boldly and sat down beside him. The chimpanzee gave him a piece of paper. Jimmy began to do just what Sammy was doing. He tore the paper across very solemnly. The chimpanzee was delighted. This was a game!

He put his arm round Jimmy's neck and bit his ear very gently. Jimmy knew that was his way of being friendly. Lilliput's monkeys did that too. He put his hand into his pocket and pulled out a small ball. He gave it to Sammy.

Sammy was thrilled. He threw the ball into the air and caught it. He threw it at Jimmy, and when Jimmy caught it and threw it back, the chimpanzee was delighted. This must be another chimpanzee come to play with him, he thought! Soon he and Jimmy were having a fine game, and Mr. Wally came to watch them. He liked to see his pet chimpanzee so happy.

"Come and play with him every day, Jimmy," said Mr. Wally. "He will love it."

"I love it too," said Jimmy, slipping out of the cage. "Isn't it a fine feeling you get when animals will play with you and be friends with you, Mr. Wally?"

"Ah—you have one of the greatest gifts in the world, young Jimmy," said Mr. Wally. "One of these days you will be famous, for you will be able to do anything you like with animals, and they will love you with all their hearts."

Jimmy went red with pleasure. Only Lotta knew how much he loved being with the animals. He was never afraid of them and they were never afraid of him. He knew what they were thinking—he knew what they were feeling. Oh, if only he had an animal of his own—one he could love and teach!

He went off to have his tea. He could smell something good cooking outside his caravan. His mother looked up.

"You seem to have grown these last few weeks, Jimmy," she said. "I believe circus-life suits you."

"Of course it does," said Jimmy. "Mother, I do think our caravan looks nice now, painted such pretty colours—and don't the new curtains look pretty at the windows?"

"Yes," said his mother. "But my word, Jimmy, I miss having rooms to move about in! If only we could have a bigger caravan—but that would cost far too much money."

"Mother, I'll buy you one some day," said Jimmy, putting his arm round his mother's waist and giving her a hug. "Dad and I will make so much money at the circus that we'll be able to give you anything you like."

"Tell Lotta that after tea I want her to come and do some lessons," said his mother, as he ate three big brown sausages. "You too, Jimmy."

"All right, Mother," said Jimmy. He liked sitting by his mother, reading to her, or writing from a book, but Lotta didn't. It was always a great business to find the little girl when lessons were anywhere about.

He ran off to find her after he had finished his meal. He saw her on the steps of her caravan, and he called to her.

"Lotta! Lotta!"

Lotta looked at him. "Coming!" she shouted, and she

ran down the steps—but she disappeared round her caravan at top speed, and when Jimmy turned round to see if she was coming she was nowhere to be seen!

Lal was peeping out of the door, laughing. "Lotta's gone to hide!" she said. "She guessed it was lessons this evening. Go and find her, Jimmy, and if she won't come, catch hold of her hair and bring her. She can't bear her hair pulled."

Jimmy went off to look for Lotta, smiling all over his face. He was beginning to learn how to treat that wild little circus-girl now. In two minutes he had found Lotta and was leading her to his mother by a handful of her dark curly hair.

"Here's a new monkey, Mother," he said. "I found her in Lilliput's caravan, behind his bed. Lilliput said she was too bad a monkey to put with his, so I brought her along to you. See if she can be as clever as Sammy, the chimpanzee, tonight!"

JIMMY GETS A DOG OF HIS OWN

The circus was doing well. When its stay at Bigchester came to an end, Mr. Galliano shared out the money with his circus-folk. Everyone was pleased, especially Mr. Brown, for he had earned much more than he had expected.

Even Jimmy was paid by Mr. Galliano. This was a surprise to him, for he had not expected to earn any money.

"You work for me—yes?" said Mr. Galliano, when he saw Jimmy's astonished face. "You care for the animals —yes? Then you must be paid."

Jimmy put his money away in a box and hid it in a special place under his caravan. It might come in useful some day when he himself performed in the circus. For that was what Jimmy had set his heart on now—he wanted to be a *real* circus-boy—one who went into the ring at night and did something clever to make the people laugh and cheer, just as Lotta did. She rode the horses and looked as beautiful as a fairy each night as she jumped from one horse to another. If only he could do something like that!

But Jimmy was not very good at riding. He would never be as good as Lotta.

"You have begun too late, Jimmy," said Laddo, Lotta's father. "I put Lotta on a horse when she was nine months old—she could ride when she was a year old. That is why she is so good now."

Jimmy thought perhaps he might be a clever acrobat like Oona. But he was too stiff. Oona said the same thing to him as Laddo had said. "You are too old to begin now, Jimmy. You walk the tight-rope quite well—but you will never be able to do all the things I do. I began when I was one year old."

Jimmy wondered if he could be a clown—but he felt sure he would never be able to say funny things quickly enough. Sticky Stanley always had a funny answer ready for everything—but Jimmy had to think quite a long time before he could say anything funny, and then perhaps it wasn't funny at all.

"Oh, well, never mind—at any rate I get on with the animals better than anyone else," thought Jimmy. "And just wait till I get a dog of my own. I'll teach it tricks that Lal has never thought of. She'll be able to take *my* dog into the ring and it will be more clever than any of hers."

Lal had not forgotten her promise to give Jimmy a puppy when she heard of a good one. One day she came to Jimmy and gave him an exciting piece of news.

"I have had a message from my brother, who lives in the next town we are going to," she said. "He always looks out for good dogs for me, and he says he has found a good little pup who will be clever at circus work. If you like to go and see him with me, I'll buy him for you if you like him."

Jimmy was thrilled. A dog of his own at last! He beamed all over his face and thanked Lal. He longed for the circus to be on the move again so that he might see the little puppy with Lal.

Soon everything was packed up once more. Sammy the chimpanzee left before the others, for Mr. Wally said his caravan was faster than the others, as it was pulled by his car. Jimmy waved to Sammy, who went off sitting beside Mr. Wally in the car, wearing a new straw hat with a blue ribbon on. Jimmy had become very fond of the chimpanzee—but he hadn't managed to teach it to clean its teeth yet.

The circus was on the road again. Down the lanes went the long procession of caravans and cages and carts, with old Jumbo in the middle as usual, plodding along

happily, swishing his tail and flapping his ears. He looked round for Jimmy. He loved having the little boy beside him. Sometimes he lifted Jimmy up to his head and the little boy travelled like that, much to the envy of all the other boys he met on the road.

They soon settled in the next big town. Jimmy was impatient to go and see the puppy that Lal had heard about. The next day, when the camp was more or less settled, Lal called to Brownie, Jimmy's father. He was making some new benches, for Mr. Galliano expected even bigger crowds here.

"Brownie! Where's Jimmy? I want to take him into the town to see the new pup."

"He's down at the stream with Jumbo," said Mr. Brown.

Lal sent Lotta for Jimmy. He led Jumbo back to his tent and fastened him to his post. Then he sped off to Lal.

They caught a tram to the town. Lal knew the place well and led him to her brother's. She went into a little sweet-shop and called loudly:

"Benjy! Here's Lal!"

A small man with ginger whiskers came running out of the back of the shop in delight. He flung his arms round Lal and hugged her.

"Back again!" he cried. "It's a whole year since I've seen you, Lal. Have you come to see the pup I told you about?"

"Yes," said Lal. "This is Jimmy, Benjy. He's with the circus. He saved a dog of mine for me when it was very ill, and I want to give him a dog of his own."

"I'll take you now," said Benjy. Jimmy liked the little man very much. He had the most twinkly eyes, and a mouth full of the whitest teeth Jimmy had ever seen. He fetched a cap and took Lal and Jimmy a good way away. He went into a small back-yard, and showed them a kennel.

"There you are," he said. "In that kennel you'll see some of the finest little dogs that can be had. The mother is with them. I'd better get Mr. Jiggs to let you look at them. The mother's a bit snappy with strangers."

Mr. Jiggs came out of his house at that moment—an untidy man with a long straw in his mouth that he chewed all the time he was talking.

"We've come to see your dogs, Jiggs," said Benjy. "This boy here wants one."

Mr. Jiggs pulled the mother-dog out of her cosy kennel, and following her came four beautiful little terriers, all with wagging tails and cocked ears.

"This is the one I thought would do for you, Lal," said Benjy, pointing to a sandy-headed dog with bright eyes.

"Yes," said Lal, running her fingers over him. "He's a fine fellow. He'll be as smart as paint. What do *you* think, Jimmy?"

Jimmy looked at the four dogs. They all looked up at him, wagging their short tails. The little boy looked at each one carefully. There was one sandy-headed one, two black-headed ones, and one that was half brown and half black, with a brown spot and a black spot on its back.

Jimmy looked at the little half-and-half one. Its eyes were soft and brown, and seemed to speak to Jimmy.

"Choose me!" the little dog's eyes seemed to say. "Choose me! *I'm* your dog! Oh, choose me, Jimmy!"

The smart little sandy-headed one rubbed against his legs like a cat. The others stood back, waiting. They all seemed to know that Jimmy was choosing one of them. The little half-and-half one gave a small whine and threw herself on Jimmy. Jimmy picked her up.

"This is the one I want," he said.

"But don't you want the smartest?" said Lal in astonishment. "That one won't learn tricks quickly."

"Yes, she will," said Jimmy, cuddling her. "I know she will. I don't know how I know, Lal—but I just know this is the dog that will learn most from me."

"Let him have the one he wants," said Lal to Mr. Jiggs, who was still chewing his straw. "This boy knows more about animals than all of us put together. He's a wizard with them! How much is it?"

Jimmy was so happy. The little dog was loving, and cuddled under Jimmy's jacket all the way back to the circus. Jimmy wondered what to call her.

He shouted for Lotta when he got back. She came running over to him. She had not been able to go with him because Laddo had wanted to teach her a new trick. She was longing to see the puppy.

"Oh, Jimmy!" she cried in delight as the little puppy peeped at her. "She's sweet! Oh, I do like her brown-and-black head. It's lucky to have an animal that is half and half. What are you going to call her?"

"You name her for me, Lotta," said Jimmy. "I simply can't think of a single name. Tell me one that is simple."

"I know! I know!" cried Lotta dancing about. "Let's call her Lucky! I'm sure she'll bring you luck, Jimmy. And it's a fine name to call—listen! Luc-ky Luc-ky! Luc-ky!"

"Yes—that's a good name," said Jimmy, pleased. "Well, Lucky, how do you like your new name and your new master?"

Lucky nearly wagged her little tail off. So the two children thought she must like both her name and her master very much indeed.

"Is she to live with our dogs?" asked Lotta.

"No," said Jimmy firmly. "She is to be my very own dog, and I shall let her sleep on my feet at night."

"She'll chew your blankets to bits," said Lotta. "Your mother will be cross."

"No, she won't," said Jimmy. "Because it's too hot for me to have blankets on now, so there's none to chew. Ha, ha!"

Lotta made a face at him and gave him a pinch. Lucky licked her hand. Jimmy put her down on the grass. She tore round and round in excitement, smelling all the smells there were, and coming back to lick Jimmy's shoes every other minute. The little boy was so pleased with his pet, the first one he had ever had. He went to show her to his mother and father.

They were pleased with Lucky too. They both liked animals, though not so much as Jimmy did.

"Mother, I'm going to pay for every single scrap of food that Lucky has," said Jimmy. "I want her to be every bit my own dog. I shall teach her all kinds of tricks."

Lucky wagged her tail and pawed Jimmy's legs. She thought Jimmy was the nicest person she had ever seen. She was only two and a half months old, but she knew the people she liked.

Jimmy had a few very happy days getting to know his new puppy. He soon found that he had been right in choosing her, for she was really clever. She tried her hardest to understand all that Jimmy said to her.

"Lucky has a wonderful memory, Lotta," said Jimmy, one evening. "Once I teach her something she never seems to forget."

"That's fine, Jimmy," said Lotta. "If an animal has a good memory that's half the battle. I guess Lucky will be famous when she's older."

Lucky had a happy life. She had plenty of good food to eat, plenty of exercise, she was well brushed each day, and had so much love and petting that her little heart almost overflowed. All the circus-folk loved the merry little puppy—and Sammy the chimpanzee simply adored her. If only she would go into his cage and play with him he was perfectly happy!

She slept with Jimmy each night, and although she didn't chew the blankets, because Jimmy had none, she chewed plenty of other things. She chewed up his slippers, and his mother's old mat, and his father's pair of socks.

But nobody really minded. She was one of the family now.

LUCKY GOES TO SCHOOL

Lucky the puppy grew fast. She was a smart little dog, bright-eyed and happy. She followed Jimmy as if she were his shadow.

"Lucky, you'll be going to school soon!" said Jimmy, patting her silky head. "You'll have to learn all sorts of things and be a clever dog."

"Wuff, wuff!" said Lucky, pretending to bite Jimmy's hand. She rolled over on her back and kicked all her legs up into the air. Lotta came over, laughing.

"Isn't she a darling?" said the little girl. "When are you going to teach her tricks, Jimmy?"

"Right away," said Jimmy; "I've got a bag of biscuits. Watch me teach Lucky to sit up and beg, Lotta!"

Lotta sat down on the steps of Jimmy's caravan and watched. Jimmy sat Lucky up straight, with her back to a box and her paws in the air.

"Sit up, sit up, sit up!" he said, in a gentle, low voice. Lucky cocked her ears. She knew that voice well — when Jimmy spoke like that he wanted her to listen hard. She stayed where she was put, with her front legs in the air.

"Good little dog," said Jimmy, and he gave Lucky a biscuit. She gobbled it down in delight.

"Do you want another biscuit?" asked Jimmy.

"Wuff, wuff, wuff!" said Lucky. She was running round the biscuit bag.

"You shall have one if you sit up, sit up, sit up!" said Jimmy. He gently put Lucky up again, so that she was begging — but this time there was no box behind her to lean on. Lucky didn't mind. She could sit up straight by herself now she knew what Jimmy meant.

She wanted to please Jimmy and she wanted a biscuit too. So she sat up straight, waving her paws in the air. "Now watch me teach Lucky to ask for a biscuit," said Jimmy to Lotta.

"Do you want a biscuit, Lucky?" said Jimmy, in his low voice. Lucky cocked her ears. She knew the word *biscuit* very well indeed!

"Wuff!" she said in delight.

"Then speak for it!" said Jimmy, holding out a biscuit. "No—sit up! Sit up! Speak for the biscuit."

"Wuff! Wuff! Wuff!" said Lucky joyfully. Jimmy threw her the biscuit and she caught it.

"I say, Jimmy! Isn't she clever!" said Lotta. "Fancy learning how to beg and how to ask for a biscuit in just one lesson."

"Yes—she's a better pupil than you are," said Jimmy. "It took you three lessons before you could say your alphabet."

Lotta made a face. "If you gave me biscuits each time, I might learn it quickly, like Lucky," she said.

"Well, it's true that Lucky has learnt this trick very quickly," said Jimmy. "But I don't expect she will remember it. I shall have to teach her all over again tomorrow. I'll make her do it a few times more for biscuits and then that will be enough lessons for today for her."

So Lucky sat up and begged a few more times and gobbled up the biscuits. Her little tail wagged hard. This was a fine way of getting biscuits!

"Now for a walk, Lucky," said Jimmy. "We'll take all the dogs too, Lotta. Lucky can run loose. She never goes very far away from me."

Off they went for a long run. When they got right out on the heathery hills the two children slipped the dogs off the lead—all but two. The rest of them were now most obedient to Jimmy's long, loud whistle and would always

116

come racing to him as soon as they heard it, no matter how many rabbits they were chasing. As for Punch, whom Jimmy had cured of a bad illness, he, like Lucky, was never far away from the boy's feet.

Jimmy and Lotta lay in the heather and talked. Jimmy was never tired of hearing all the tales of the circus-folk.

She was talking about elephants now. "You know, Jimmy," she said, "elephants have longer memories than any other animals. They never forget or forgive an unkind deed."

"What! Do you mean to say that old Jumbo would remember that Harry, who ran off with the circus-money weeks ago, was unkind to him?" said Jimmy.

"Yes, he remembers it," said Lotta. "And if he saw Harry again he would try to pay him out for the unkind things he did to him."

"And does Jumbo remember the kind things that people do?" said Jimmy.

"Of course," said Lotta. "For instance, if you left the circus now, Jimmy, and didn't come back till you were grown-up, Jumbo would know you and give you just as big a welcome as he gives you now. He never forgets a friend and he never forgets an enemy."

"I can't understand anyone being unkind to animals," said Jimmy. "They trust you so—and they all have such lovely, friendly eyes."

"Yes, haven't they," said Lotta looking into Lucky's soft brown eyes. "Perhaps, Jimmy, the people that don't love animals haven't ever looked right into their eyes."

Lucky licked Lotta's nose. "You're just one big lick," said Lotta, wiping her nose. "You ought to have been called Licky, not Lucky."

Jimmy laughed. "You do say funny things Lotta," he said. "Come on—it's time to go back, Lucky! Bark for the other dogs."

Lucky lifted up her little black-brown head and barked her small puppy-bark. The children laughed. "Isn't she obedient," said Jimmy, pleased. He whistled loudly. From far and near came the sound of padding paws, and soon the ten terriers, with Lucky running round them, were trotting happily back to the circus. On the way they passed a lady with a fat, puffy wire-haired terrier.

She stood and watched the circus-dogs go by. "Poor little dogs," she said. "What a dreadful life they must lead in that circus! Look, Tinker-dog—how lucky you are to live with me, and not in a circus."

Jimmy and Lotta didn't say a word when they passed the lady. But as soon as they were safely by, Lotta burst out in a rage.

"How dare she say such a thing! Can't she see how happy and well-cared for all our dogs are? Can't she see their bright eyes and cocked ears and wagging tails?"

"No, I don't suppose she can," said Jimmy. "Her poor dog is over-fed, and looks as if he had chocolates all day long. He was fat and waddley. If she only knew it, *her* dog is to be pitied, not ours."

They were soon back at the circus camp. They put the dogs into their big kennel-cage, and gave them a feed of biscuits. Lucky smelt them and wanted some too. She knew that she would have to wait till the other dogs were fed, and she wondered how to get something to eat quickly. She remembered how Jimmy had given her biscuits for begging.

Mr. Tonks, the elephant keeper, was sitting nearby, eating some bread and cheese. Lucky ran up to him. She sat up on her hind-legs, and waved her front ones in the air.

"Wuff!" she said. "Wuff!"

Mr. Tonks laughed. "Hey, Jimmy!" he shouted. "Look at your pup. She's begging for my dinner."

Lotta and Jimmy stared in surprise. Lucky still sat up, begging, wuffing loudly.

"Well! If she isn't the smartest little dog!" said Lotta. "She's trying her trick on Tonky."

Jimmy was pleased. Lucky was even more clever than he had thought. What fun it was going to be to teach that bright little dog all kinds of things! Lucky should go to school with him every day, and he would teach her patiently and gently so that in the days to come she might go into the circus-ring at night too, and do tricks to amuse the people watching.

So, day after day, Jimmy and Lucky worked together.

The little dog loved her lessons. She was so bright and sometimes guessed what Jimmy meant her to do before he even showed her. In a week she could sit perfectly still with a biscuit on her nose until Jimmy said "Paid for!" and then she would throw it up into the air and catch it. All the usual tricks that ordinary household dogs learn, Jimmy taught Lucky in a few days. Then he began to teach her others.

She walked easily on her hind legs. She carried a flag. She wheeled a little wooden pram with Lotta's doll in it and even learnt to tuck up the doll. Jimmy's father made the pram for Lucky, and it had a special handle so that her doggy paws could push it easily.

The circus-folk laughed when they saw Lucky wheeling the pram about the camp. They gave her biscuits for it, and at last Jimmy had to keep the pram away from Lucky, for whenever she wanted a biscuit she would get it out and wheel it round the caravans.

"Jimmy, that pup of yours will make your fortune one day—yes?" said Mr. Galliano, laughing. "When is she going into the ring?"

"Not yet," said Jimmy. "I want to teach her a few more things first. Have you seen her with Sammy the chimpanzee, Mr. Galliano? They are very funny together."

Mr. Galliano went over to Sammy's big cage with Jimmy. Jimmy let the little dog in and Sammy ran to Lucky in delight. He picked up the little dog and nursed it like a baby. Then he and Lucky played 'catch' and tore round the cage in excitement. Jimmy passed Sammy a paper hat and Sammy caught Lucky and put it on her head. Mr. Galliano laughed.

"A clever little dog," he said. "She shall go into the ring one night with Lal—yes?"

Mr. Galliano went off, his hat well on one side. He always wore it like that these days, for the circus was doing well. Huge crowds came to see Mr. Wally and Sammy each night, for the clever chimpanzee amused everyone very much.

Jimmy slipped into the chimpanzee's cage and had a game with him. He picked Lucky up in his arms and whispered into the little dog's ear: "Did you hear what Mr. Galliano said? He said you could go into the ring one night and do your tricks for everyone to see. That will be a proud night for you and me, Lucky."

Jimmy was not only teaching Lucky, but he was trying his best to teach Sammy the only trick that Mr. Wally couldn't seem to teach him — he was teaching him to clean his teeth. And how did Jimmy do it? Why, he found out that Sammy simply loved the taste of aniseed, and so he rubbed the toothbrush with oil of aniseed. When Sammy smelt the aniseed and tasted it, he was thrilled, and would rub his teeth with the brush as long as ever Jimmy would let him.

Mr. Wally was pleased when he found that Jimmy had taught the chimpanzee this. He gave Jimmy fifty pence and the little boy put it into the old box where he kept his savings. He had a lot of money there now.

He did not know how soon he would spend it all!

MR. WALLY HAS AN ACCIDENT

The days went happily by. The circus was having a marvellous time, for Galliano's beautiful horses were famous, and so were Lilliput's clever little monkeys. Everyone loved Lal's dogs too. But it was Mr. Wally's chimpanzee that drew the biggest crowds. There had been many clever chimpanzees before, but not one quite so human as Sammy.

Mr. Wally was making a lot of money, for Mr. Galliano paid him well. He bought himself a new little car to pull his caravan, and when it arrived he called all the circus-folk to see it.

They stood round the little red car admiringly. Mr. Wally was the only one of them who owned a car.

"Who's coming for a ride in it?" said Mr. Wally. "It's very fast—one of the best cars to be got nowadays. Now then—who's for a ride?"

But nobody seemed to want a ride. The circus-folk were used to going slowly in their caravans and nobody but Mr. Wally got very excited about cars. One by one the people looking on melted away, back to their work, and only Jimmy was left.

"Would *you* like to come, Jimmy?" asked Mr. Wally.

"I'd love to, Mr. Wally," said Jimmy eagerly. But just then his father called him.

"Jimmy! You've got to help me this morning. There's a job here that needs two pairs of hands."

"Oh," said Jimmy in disappointment. "I'm so sorry, Mr. Wally."

"I'll take Sammy," said Mr. Wally. "He always likes a car-ride. Go and get him for me, Jimmy."

122

Jimmy fetched Sammy from his cage. He was dressed as usual in trousers and coat and straw hat. The big chimpanzee was delighted to go out with his beloved master. He knew the car was a new one and he ran his hairy paw over the smooth paint in delight. Sammy loved bright colours, especially red.

"Get in, Sammy," said Mr. Wally, settling himself behind the steering-wheel. Sammy leapt lightly over the door and sat down beside Mr. Wally in the front seat. He could open doors quite well, but it was easier to jump over them.

"Good-bye, Sammy!" said Jimmy. Sammy waved his paw. "R-r-r-r-r-r-r-r!" went the engine of the car, and the little red thing set off across the bumpy circus-field and out of the big gate.

Jimmy went to help his father. He worked hard all morning. He went to have a look at the chimpanzee as he was going to have his dinner—but to his surprise Sammy was not back.

"Where's Sammy?" he called to Mr. Tonks, who was oiling Jumbo to make him sleek and shining.

"He hasn't come back," said Mr. Tonks. "Mr. Galliano's getting worried. Wally should have been back two hours ago."

Just as Jimmy was sitting down outside his caravan to eat two big sausages that his mother had cooked for him, he saw a telegram-boy coming in at the gate. Jimmy's heart stood still. Was it from Mr. Wally? Had there been an accident?

The boy took the telegram to Mr. Galliano's caravan. Jimmy ran to him. Mr. Galliano tore open the telegram and frowned.

"No answer," he said to the boy. "Look here!" he called to Mrs. Galliano. "Wally's had an accident with that new car of his. He's broken his leg—and Sammy's disappeared!

Now what are we to do? I am *so* worried."

Jimmy stared in dismay when he heard this. Mr. Wally with a broken leg—and Sammy gone! He must have been frightened in the accident and run away. Poor old Sammy!

"Now we'll have the people scared for miles around because the chimpanzee's lost," grumbled Mr. Galliano. "And there's Wally in hospital with a broken leg—he can't possibly go after Sammy—and what in the world shall we do when we *do* find Sammy! He can't go into the ring without his keeper."

Jimmy felt something licking his hand. It was Lucky. An idea flashed into the little boy's head. Could Lucky find Sammy for him? He had already taught the little dog how to find all kinds of things. He had only to say. "I've lost my handkerchief!" for Lucky to go and hunt for it till she found it. And if he said, "I've lost my purse," or "I've lost my knife," the puppy would run off to hunt at once. If it was any word she knew, Lucky would hunt till she found what was lost.

"Suppose I took her to where the accident happened," thought Jimmy. "And suppose I said to her, 'I've lost Sammy!' Would she be clever enough to find the chimpanzee, I wonder?"

He went up the caravan steps to ask Mr. Galliano. But Mr. Galliano was too worried even to listen to Jimmy. He waved to him to go away.

"I just wanted to know if I could go and . . ." began Jimmy. But Mr. Galliano roared at him angrily.

"You will not go anywhere—no! Wally goes—and he does not come back, and Sammy is lost! Nobody will go anywhere today! You will stay in the camp!"

Jimmy went off, disappointed. It was no use asking Mr. Galliano again. Lotta ran over to him, and he told her about Mr. Wally's accident and how Sammy had run away.

"I thought if I could take Lucky to the place where the accident happened and tell her Sammy was lost, perhaps she'd find him," said Jimmy. "But Mr. Galliano won't let me go out of the camp today—or anybody else either."

"Pooh!" said Lotta. "We'll go, all the same."

Jimmy stared at the untidy little girl. "We can't disobey Mr. Galliano," he said. "I daren't."

"Well, if *you're* afraid of him, *I'm* not!" said Lotta. "I shall take Lucky myself, and see if she can find Sammy."

"You're not to," said Jimmy fiercely. "Lucky is my dog. Nobody else is to take her about but me."

"Well, if you won't come I shall *have* to take her," said Lotta, her eyes flashing angrily. "You're a coward, Jimmy! You daren't do something you know is the only thing to do, because you're afraid of disobeying Mr. Galliano. I don't care if he whips me, I'm going to find poor old Sammy! Think of him hiding away somewhere, scared out of his life, and perhaps being shot by somebody who is afraid of him."

Jimmy jumped up, alarmed. "Shot!" he said. "Surely nobody would shoot dear old Sammy!"

"'Course they would," said Lotta. "It's all very well to come and see a chimpanzee in a circus when his keeper is with him—but who wants to meet a chimpanzee down a lane or in their back garden? Nobody, outside of circus or Zoo-folks! Lucky! Lucky! Come with me. Good-bye Jimmy."

"I'm coming too," said Jimmy. "I'm not a coward, Lotta. I just didn't think of all that might happen. I do see that we've got to go, even if it means disobeying Mr. Galliano. But how shall we go—and where?"

"I'll get Laddo to find out where the accident happened," said Lotto. "If it's a good way off, we'll go on Beauty, my own horse. She can take us both quite easily."

In a minute or two Lotta had found out where the

accident had happened. "It's not very far off," she said. "It happened at cross-roads at Bentonville. That's six miles away. Go and get Beauty, Jimmy, and I'll keep watch and see that no one sees you."

Everything went well. The circus-folk were all gathered round Galliano's caravan, whilst he told them about Mr. Wally and Sammy, and discussed with them what they were to do in the show that night, to take the place of Mr. Wally's turn with Sammy. There was not even a groom with the horses.

Lotta and Jimmy slipped out of a little gate at the farther end of the field. Beauty was a strong, sleek white horse, Lotta's very own, She easily carried the two children. Lucky, who had never been on horseback before, was surprised to be jogged up and down, but so long as she felt Jimmy's arm round her she did not mind anything. They went off quietly down the lane. They came to the main road. There was a grassy edge to the road and Beauty cantered along this happily. When the children came to a sign-post they looked at it to see the way to Bentonville.

Lotta could not read the name, but Jimmy could, of course. "You'd probably have gone the wrong way, Lotta, if you'd been silly and gone off without me," said Jimmy. "You wouldn't have been able to read the sign properly."

"I shall do my reading lessons better now," said Lotta. "It would have been dreadful if I couldn't have gone the right way."

Beauty began to gallop. Jimmy was quite at home on horseback now and he enjoyed the ride. Lucky whined a little. She thought it was all very strange indeed.

On and on they went to Bentonville and at last they got there. They found themselves at cross-roads and then they knew that they had come to the right place, for there, by the side of the road, was Mr. Wally's lovely new red car, with the side wing bent and broken, and the glass splintered.

"We needn't ask anybody anything," whispered Lotta. "Just get down and let Lucky nose about, Jimmy. She may smell where Sammy went."

Jimmy jumped down and let Lucky run round for a while and then he called the little dog to him. He took her head in his hands and looked down into her bright eyes.

"Lucky," he said, in the low, gentle voice that always made Lucky listen hard, "I've lost Sammy! Sammy! I've lost Sammy! Where's Sammy! I've lost Sammy!"

Lucky cocked her ears and gave a little whine. She understood perfectly. Sammy was gone and had to be found. She could find Jimmy's handkerchief and his purse and his knife by smelling them out when they were lost—and now she must find Sammy. She nosed about to see if she could find a Sammy-smell. She ran round and about the road. No Sammy-smell there. She ran to the side. No Sammy-smell there! She ran through a hole in the hedge, on the side where the car was—and there, in the field, Lucky found a Sammy-smell! Yes—there was no doubt about it! Sammy had leapt right out of the car, over the hedge and into the field!

"Lotta! Will you wait here whilst I go after Lucky?" said Jimmy in excitement. "She's found the right smell, I do believe—and she'll follow it till she comes to Sammy!"

"Yes, I'll wait with Beauty," said Lotta. "I'll take her into this field."

Jimmy set off after Lucky. Lucky was nosing along, following the strong Sammy-smell. Jimmy was thrilled. This was his own idea! Surely Mr. Galliano would not be *very* angry with him for being disobedient if only he brought back Sammy safe and sound?

And now, where *was* Sammy?

WHAT HAPPENED TO SAMMY
THE CHIMPANZEE

Lucky had picked up Sammy's footprints with her clever nose—but the chimpanzee was a long way away! He had jumped right over the hedge, sprinted over the field, got into a lane that led up a hill and had gone down the other side, frightened out of his life.

Sammy had been sitting quietly in the car beside Mr. Wally when the accident happened. Another car had run into theirs at the cross-roads, and there had been such a loud crash that Sammy had got the shock of his life. He did not wait to see what Mr. Wally was doing or saying—he just jumped and fled.

As he ran up the hill he met two woodmen walking together. When they saw the chimpanzee coming they stared as if they couldn't believe their eyes.

"Ooh! What is it?" said one.

"It's a monkey, isn't it?" said the other.

"No—an ape," said the first man. "My word—what's it doing?"

Sammy stopped when he saw the two men. Into his frightened mind came the thought that perhaps these men would help him. He ambled up to them—but they tore off in terror, dropping their bags behind them.

Sammy was frightened of their shouts. He did not go after them, but he ran up to their bags. He smelt something good inside—the men's dinner!

It was ham sandwiches, buns, and apples. Sammy picked up the food, ran to the hedge and crouched there. He ate everything in the bags, and most of all he liked the apples.

As he sat there a woman came up the hill. Sammy thought she looked kind, rather like Lotta's mother, whom he knew very well. He ran out of the hedge towards her, making a funny chattering noise—his way of asking for help. He wanted to get back to Mr. Wally. He felt strange with no friends around him.

The woman gave a yell and raced down the hill at top speed. She met a man and he asked her what was the matter.

"Oh, it's a chimpanzee!" she gasped.

"Nonsense!" said the man, patting her on the back. "There are no chimpanzees here—only rabbits and foxes."

"I tell you it *was* a chimpanzee," said the woman. But the man still shook his head. And at that very moment Sammy appeared, trotting down the hill towards them. He thought perhaps the man might be a friend of his. The man gave a shout.

"You're right!" he said to the woman. "It *is* a chimpanzee! Quick! Get into this house!"

They ran into a house. Poor Sammy! He was so disappointed when they disappeared and shut the door. He was lonely. He wanted Mr. Wally very badly.

He went into the garden and looked around to see if he could find anyone there. The man and the woman and two other people were watching him from a window.

"I'll telephone to the police," said the man. "It's an escaped chimpanzee. He ought to be shot."

"Poor thing," said the woman. "I saw him at the circus the other night. I expect the circus-folk are looking for him."

"Well, he can't be allowed to go roaming the country-side," said the man. "I'll tell the police to get guns and go after him."

Sammy did not hear all this, and he would not have

understood it if he had. He sniffed round the doors, tried to open them, decided that he couldn't, and went off up the hill again. He went over the top and down into a small village. There he ran into some little children. They did not know what he was and they stood and stared at him in surprise. Sammy loved children. He made his little chattering noise and held out his hand to a boy.

The little chap put his hand into the chimpanzee's. Sammy was delighted. Here was a friend at last. He stroked the little boy's hair. Then he began to do some of his tricks. He was still dressed in his trousers and coat, but he had lost his hat. He took off his clothes and pretended to go to sleep under a bush. Then he yawned, stretched himself and got up. He dressed himself and then pretended to wash and clean his teeth and brush his hair.

The children crowded round him in delight. What a clever animal! Sammy was pleased. He hugged a little girl gently, and began to play with the children.

But it was not for long. A woman, looking out of the window to see if her children were all right, caught sight of Sammy and stared in astonishment and fear.

"Johnny — Ellen — come indoors at once!" she shouted.

"Oh, Mummy, but we want to play with this queer animal," cried Johnny.

"Come in *at once*!" shouted his mother.

Soon the street was deserted, for all the children ran home and left Sammy. The next thing he saw was a little crowd of men, carrying sticks and iron bars, coming towards him. Sammy did not know that they were coming to hit him. He ran towards them happily, thinking he might play with them too. One of the men stopped and took aim at Sammy. He threw an iron bar at the chimpanzee — but Sammy dodged, held up his hand and neatly caught it. He thought this was a new game, and he threw the iron bar back at the men.

Luckily it did not hit anyone. The men stopped in surprise. "It's no good throwing things at him," said one. "He'll only throw them back. Try to get him into a corner and then we'll catch him all right."

So the men spread out into a ring and gradually surrounded Sammy. The chimpanzee was not taking any notice of them for a moment. He had seen something standing by a wall that interested him — a bicycle! Sammy rode his own bicycle every night in the circus-ring and he knew bicycles well. Whilst he was looking at this one, the men got nearer and nearer.

Sammy looked up. He suddenly became frightened. He did not like the look of these silent men coming nearer and nearer. How could he get away? What was he to do?

And what do you suppose he did? Why, he jumped suddenly on the bicycle, pedalled away hard and rode straight at the men. They were so startled that they got out of his way.

Through the crowd cycled Sammy, right down the village street and away beyond. He waved his hand to the astonished men. He was pleased with himself. He liked the new bicycle. It was bigger than his own, but he could manage it quite well. On and on he went, and soon came to another village.

But here a policeman with a gun was waiting for Sammy. Someone had telephoned from the other village and told him to be ready for Sammy. Sammy had no idea what a gun was. He pedalled straight at the blue policeman.

Bang! The gun went off. It made a sound rather like the crack of Mr. Galliano's whip. Sammy was used to that— but something warned him that the gun the policeman held was not the same as the circus whip whose sound he knew so well. The chimpanzee jumped off his bicycle and ran into a garden. He crouched as he ran, for he was afraid of the gun. He came to a small shed at the back. He leapt in through a window and hid himself under some sacks. He lay there as still as could be.

And what was Jimmy doing all this time? Ah, Jimmy was getting hot and out of breath, for Lucky was dragging him on her lead across fields, down a lane, up a hill and down again and into a village. There he met the parents of the children that Sammy had played with, and they told him Sammy had been there. Lucky sniffed down the village street, but lost the scent.

"My dog can't seem to smell him any more," said Jimmy, in despair. "I wonder why that is."

"Well, the chimpanzee went off on my bicycle," said a butcher's boy. "So I guess that's why your dog can't smell his tracks any more. He went towards the next village. We've just telephoned there to the policeman, and he is waiting for the chimp with a gun."

Jimmy went pale, though his cheeks were as hot as fire. Oh, surely, surely, no one would shoot dear, gentle clever old Sammy!

"Come on, Lucky, we must go as fast as we can!" cried Jimmy, and off went the two along the road to the next village. When they came there, Jimmy saw a crowd in the road.

"Have you seen the chimpanzee?" he panted.

"Yes," said a man, pointing towards a nearby garden. "He went there. He's hiding in a shed. The policeman is just going to undo the door and shoot him."

"Oh, he mustn't—he mustn't!" cried Jimmy. "He's a wonderful creature, and wouldn't harm anyone. Quick, Lucky, quick!"

They forced their way through the crowd and went round the house to the back. There were five men round a small shed. The policeman was just about to open the door and shoot into the sacks that covered Sammy. The men had looked through the window and had seen that

Sammy was hiding under the heap of sacks.

"You are not to hurt our chimpanzee!" shouted Jimmy. "He's quite harmless, and is the cleverest in the world! He is worth hundreds of pounds. Let me go to him."

The men stared at the little boy in surprise. "What! Go into the shed with that chimpanzee!" said the policeman.

"Of course," said Jimmy. "I love him, and so do all the circus-folk. He's just like a human being!"

Just then Lucky managed to squeeze herself under the door of the shed. She ran to the heap of sacks and barked happily. Here was Sammy, her friend, at last! Sammy popped his head up, picked up the little dog and cuddled her lovingly. The men looking in through the window saw this and were amazed.

Jimmy opened the door and went into the shed. "Sammy! Sammy! Here's Jimmy come for you!" he cried. The chimpanzee leapt up and ran to Jimmy in delight. He chattered away in joy, stroking Jimmy's head and patting his shoulder. He put his arm round the little boy and hugged him. The men who were watching were full of astonishment.

"There you are!" said Jimmy happily. "What did I tell you? He is gentle and tame, and as clever as can be. I'll take him back to the circus with me now."

"No, you'd better wait for a van to come," said the policeman. But Jimmy wouldn't. He guessed that nobody would try to part him from the chimpanzee. He marched out into the road with Sammy, holding the big chimpanzee by the paw, and back the three of them went up the road — Jimmy, Sammy, and Lucky. Everyone followed them in astonishment.

"What a boy!" said the policeman. "Never saw anyone like him in my life! Went in and took that chimp's hand as cool as you please!"

It took Jimmy and Sammy a good while to get back to

Lotta. The little girl was still patiently waiting with Beauty, her horse. She was full of joy when at last she saw Jimmy coming with Sammy and Lucky.

"I was only just in time, Lotta," said Jimmy, and he told her the story as they cantered home. Sammy sat between Lotta and Jimmy, perfectly happy and good. He held Lucky in his arms.

They rode through the circus-gate. "What do you suppose Mr. Galliano will say when he sees us?" said Jimmy nervously, seeing Mr. Galliano in the distance, with his top-hat perfectly straight up on his head.

JIMMY GOES INTO THE RING

When the circus-folk saw Jimmy and Lotta riding on Beauty, the lovely white horse, with Sammy in the middle, they were amazed. Mr. Galliano suddenly saw them too, and his big cigar dropped right out of his mouth.

Jimmy rode up to him. "Please, sir," he said, "we disobeyed you. You said no one was to leave the camp today, but Lotta and I did, with Lucky. We felt so certain we could find Sammy and bring him back."

"You young scamp," said Mr. Galliano, with a terrible frown—but Jimmy saw that his eyes were twinkling under his eyebrows. "How dare you disobey the great Galliano? And you too, Lotta—you ought to know better—yes?"

"Wuff, wuff!" said Lucky, trying to get out of Sammy's arms—but the chimpanzee held her tight.

"Get down, take Sammy to his cage, give him a few bananas and come to see me in my caravan," said Mr. Galliano. The two children hurried to do as they were told. No one asked them anything, for they knew that the story must be told to Mr. Galliano first.

Sammy was soon happily eating bananas in his cage. Lucky was crunching up biscuits beside him. Jimmy and Lotta hurried to Mr. Galliano's caravan. Mrs. Galliano was there too. She shut the door behind them.

Jimmy told his story and Mr. Galliano listened.

"You have a gift for rescuing runaway animals—yes?" he said, with a laugh. "First the elephant, and now the chimpanzee. You are a naughty boy to disobey, Jimmy, but you are a good boy, yes, to save Sammy. But we cannot let Sammy go into the ring alone. He is useless without Wally."

A wonderful idea came into Jimmy's head. "Please, sir, let *me* go into the ring with him," begged the little boy earnestly. "He will do as much for me as he does with Mr. Wally. Really he will. I've played games with him and practised with him every day. And I taught him to clean his teeth, though Mr. Wally couldn't. Do, do let me."

Mr. Galliano stared at Jimmy and then looked across at Mrs. Galliano.

She nodded her head. "Jimmy is a good boy with animals," she said. "A very good boy. You let him do this, Galliano. I and his mother will begin at once to make him a fine suit for tonight."

Jimmy could have hugged Mrs. Galliano. He was wild with joy. To go into the big circus-ring at last! To be there in fine clothes, under the glaring lights, with hundreds of people watching and clapping! Could anything be more exciting!

"Tell your mother to come here," said Mr. Galliano, lighting another big cigar. "You know what to do exactly, Jimmy—yes? We will have a practice this afternoon with Sammy. Be ready in ten minutes' time."

Whilst Mrs. Galliano and Mrs. Brown were cutting out red knickerbockers and a fine yellow coat with a blue waistcoat for Jimmy to wear that night, Jimmy was practising with Sammy for that night's show. He took Sammy into the ring, with all the necessary things—the cot, the chair, the table, the bowl of water, the bicycle and everything—and under Mr. Galliano's sharp eye the little boy went through the whole turn just as he had so often seen Mr. Wally do.

Sammy loved doing his tricks with Jimmy. He loved his master, Mr. Wally, but there was something about this little boy, with his bright deep eyes and his low, gentle voice that Sammy understood and adored. He would willingly have died for Jimmy.

"Good, good, good," said Mr. Galliano, when the turn was finished. "You are a proper circus-boy—yes."

What a scramble it was to get Jimmy's things finished in time—and how grand he looked when he got into his red knickerbockers, his yellow coat and blue waistcoat. He wore a round gold cap and blue stockings. He looked almost as grand as Mr. Galliano himself. What a good thing he had saved up his money! When Lotta saw him she stared without saying a word.

"Well, do I look nice?" asked Jimmy impatiently.

"Oh, Jimmy! You look simply grand," said Lotta. "I don't feel as if I shall ever dare to make a face at you again."

But as the cheeky little girl immediately made one of her very worst faces at him, she couldn't have meant what she said!

Jimmy felt a bit nervous when the time came for him to take Sammy into the ring. There were crowds of people there that night to see the chimpanzee, for everyone had heard of his adventures that day. Sammy was delighted to have Jimmy going into the ring with him. He did not seem to miss Mr. Wally at all.

He did everything just as he should—but in the middle of it all, what do you suppose happened?

Why, Lucky escaped from her kennel and tore into the big tent to find her little master. She raced straight into the ring, barking madly. Jimmy stared in dismay.

"Go back, Lucky, go back!" he said. But Lucky was too excited to listen. She had had a thrilling day and she meant to play with Jimmy and Sammy, and not go back to her kennel.

Mr. Galliano cracked his whip. That meant that Jimmy was to go on with his turn. He did hope that Lucky wouldn't spoil it! Wouldn't that be too bad, his very first night in the ring?

Sammy was just dressing himself after getting out of the cot. He was about to sit down and wash when Lucky dashed up to him. Sammy looked down at his small playmate. He lifted her up on his knee, and—whatever do you think he did?

He washed Lucky's face for her, cleaned her teeth, and brushed her hair. Oh dear, how everyone shouted and laughed! Lucky didn't like it at all and she tried to get away, but Sammy held her tightly. Then he washed his own face, cleaned his teeth and did his hair.

When the time came for him to ride off to school, Sammy jumped nimbly on his bicycle with Lucky still tucked under one arm. How everyone cheered! They did not know that this was all Sammy's own idea—they thought the chimpanzee had been taught to play with Lucky like this.

When the turn came to an end and Jimmy went off with Sammy and Lucky, the people cheered till they were hoarse, and Jimmy had to come back three times with Sammy and bow. He was so delighted that the tears came into his eyes and he had to blink them back. Good old Sammy! Good old Lucky! They had both done their very best for him that night.

Mr. Galliano was delighted with Jimmy. He told him that he could do the turn in the ring with Sammy and Lucky every night till Mr. Wally was ready to come back. Then perhaps Mr. Wally would let Jimmy help him.

So night after night Jimmy took Sammy into the ring and the chimpanzee grinned to hear the clapping and cheering he got—and when Lucky came dashing into the ring at exactly the right moment to be washed and brushed by Sammy, the people clapped all the more.

Jimmy's days were very full now. He had to practise a good deal with Sammy and Lucky, besides helping Lotta with the other dogs, and giving Mr. Tonks a hand with Jumbo. He practised his riding too, and could now walk the tight-rope just as well as Oona the acrobat could. He was teaching the clever little Lucky as many tricks as he could whilst she was young and eager, for he knew that is the best time for any animal to learn. So, from dawn to dusk Jimmy was busy, and his mother said she hardly ever saw him except at meal-times.

Mr. Wally had been pleased to hear that Sammy had been found and rescued. But he was not so pleased to hear that Sammy would go into the ring each night with Jimmy and do just as well with the little boy as he did with him, his trainer and master.

Nobody thought that Mr. Wally would be jealous of

139

Jimmy. Everyone was quite sure that when Mr. Wally's leg was better he would tell Jimmy that he might help him in the ring each night with Sammy and Lucky.

But everybody was wrong. When Mr. Wally came back to the circus, limping slightly, he watched Jimmy and Sammy in the ring for one night. And then he went to Mr. Galliano.

"Mr. Galliano, sir," he said, "tomorrow night I take Sammy into the ring myself. I am quite better now."

"That is good, yes," said Mr. Galliano. "You will like Jimmy to help you, Wally—he is a very good boy."

"I won't want him to help me," said Mr. Wally. "He is a good boy with animals, but I do not want him to come into the ring with me when I take Sammy there. Sammy is mine and I trained him. No one else shall share him in the ring when I am there."

Mr. Galliano was angry. "Jimmy did a great deal for Sammy and you should be grateful, yes," he shouted. "It is not much to ask that he should help you. The boy loves to go into the ring."

"I *am* grateful to Jimmy," said Mr. Wally firmly, "and I shall pay him well for all the time he has been taking Sammy into the ring for me. But he shall not share Sammy in the ring now I am back. And if you tell me I must take him into the ring, Mr. Galliano, then I will go away with Sammy and you will not see me again."

Mr. Wally went out of the caravan. He knew quite well he had beaten Mr. Galliano. Mr. Galliano could not afford to let him go just when the chimpanzee was drawing such big crowds to the circus every night. Mr. Galliano sat and thought. Then he shouted for Jimmy.

He told the little boy what Mr. Wally had said. Jimmy was surprised and upset. Not go into the ring any more, just when he had got used to it and loved it so! He stood and stared at Mr. Galliano in dismay. "Am I not to go into the ring *any* more?" he asked, his voice trembling a little.

"Some day perhaps, yes," said Mr. Galliano. "But not now. There is nothing you can do except with Sammy, and Mr. Wally will not have that."

Jimmy went to his own caravan, sad and disappointed. How horrid of Mr. Wally! He sat down on the big bed and thought about it. His mother found him there, his bright face looking miserable for once.

"What's the matter, Jimmy?" she said in alarm. Jimmy told her. His mother put her arm around him and squeezed him.

"Jimmy, you mustn't mind when things go wrong," she said. "You have been a lucky boy in many things lately. Now that an obstacle has come and you can't get what you want, don't worry about it. The best way to treat obstacles is to use them as stepping-stones. Laugh at them, tread on them, and let them lead you to something better. As for Mr. Wally, don't think hardly of him. He loves Sammy, and it's quite natural that he should want him all to himself in the ring. You wouldn't like any one to share Lucky with you, would you?"

"No, I shouldn't, Mother," said Jimmy, feeling much better already. "You're a darling, Mother — you just say the right things. I won't worry about this, and I won't be horrid to Mr. Wally. I'll do as you say and make this obstacle into a stepping-stone to something better."

And how did Jimmy do that? Ah, you will soon see.

GOOD OLD LUCKY

Jimmy ran to find Lotta to tell her that Mr. Wally would not let him help in the ring with Sammy any more. Lotta was angry.

"Nasty, horrid Mr. Wally," she said fiercely. "I'll creep into his caravan tonight whilst he is in the ring and put butter into his tin of paraffin and empty his tea into his cocoa-tin and . . ."

"Lotta! You mustn't say things like that!" said Jimmy, astonished. "You would be more horrid than Mr. Wally if you did that. Don't be silly."

Lotta stared at Jimmy, surprised. "But aren't you angry with Mr. Wally too?" she asked.

"I was," said Jimmy. "But I'm not now. You know, Lotta, my mother says when obstacles come it is best to tread on them and use them as stepping-stones to something better. I don't know how I'm going to do it, but I shall have a try. If I can't go into the ring one way I shall find another."

"Good for you," said Lotta, giving Jimmy a hug. "Look —there's Mr. Wally going to feed Sammy. He's not looking at us. I expect he thinks you are angry with him."

"Well, he won't think that for long," said Jimmy. "Hie, Mr. Wally! Can I help you to feed Sammy?"

Mr. Wally turned in surprise and looked at the bright-faced little boy. He had expected him to be sulky and rude to him. For a moment he didn't know what to do.

"All right," he said. "You can feed him. Thanks very much. I'm busy and could do with a bit of help."

"I'll clean out his cage too," said Jimmy, and ran off cheerfully to get a pail and broom. Mr. Wally stared after him. He had never known a boy behave like that before when something horrid had happened. "All the same, he is *not* going into the ring with Sammy and me," said Mr. Wally to himself.

One day, when Jimmy was practising walking the tight-rope under Oona's sharp eye, Lucky came up. The little dog watched her master balancing carefully on the rope, and cocked her head on one side.

"Wuff!" she said, which meant "I'll have a try too!" And before Jimmy could say a word, Lucky gave a spring and landed with three legs on the rope. She fell off again at once, but she didn't care a bit. No—up she went again, and this time she got all four legs on, one behind the other. How funny she looked, to be sure. She stood there, swaying, and then jumped down. Oona and Jimmy stared at her. Whatever *would* Lucky do next?

"Jimmy!" said Oona suddenly. "I believe you could teach that dog of yours to walk the tight-rope. She is as clever as ten terriers rolled into one. Here, Lucky! Let's have a look at your paws."

Lucky ran to Oona and put up a paw. She really seemed to know everything that was said to her. Even Lal said she had never met a dog like Lucky. Oona looked carefully at her hard pads.

"See, Jimmy," he said to the little boy. "A dog has good strong pads, divided into pieces—and if I made Lucky a thin rubber sock to wear on each foot I believe she could grasp the tight-rope well, and get a fine grip. I say! A dog that walked the tight-rope! Such a thing has never been heard of before."

Jimmy listened with wide eyes and flushed cheeks. He petted Lucky and stroked her silky head. How glad he was he had chosen her and not one of the other puppies he had seen!

"I'll make the rubber socks today," said Oona, as

excited as Jimmy. "We'll see how they work. Lucky would have to wear something—her feet are not quite right for this sort of work."

Well, Oona kept his word. He got some thin white rubber, and with strong gum he shaped them into socks to fit Lucky's small paws. When Lucky had them on she did not seem to mind at all. Oona had been afraid she might bite them off.

"Now bring her to the tight-rope in the ring," said Oona excitedly. "Nobody's there just now. We'll have it all to ourselves."

So they took Lucky to the ring, and put up the tight-rope there. Jimmy ran along the rope lightly, and whistled to Lucky. "Come up, then, come up!" he called. Lucky did not have to be told twice. Up she sprang and stood on the rope with all four feet. The rubber socks gave her a fine grip. She tried to walk a step, missed her footing and fell off. But up she went again and again—and again! Lucky loved trying new things, and her greatest joy was to try and do what her little master did. At the end of twenty minutes she had learnt to keep her balance and to walk three steps.

Oona and Jimmy were too excited to say a word. They just looked at one another in glee.

"Wuff!" said Lucky, and licked Jimmy's hand. Then Jimmy found his tongue—but not to lick with. He poured out all his hopes and plans to Oona—how he would teach Lucky marvellous things, and the little dog would be famous—and he, Jimmy, would take her into the ring each night and show the people what a wonderful dog he had! Oona listened and nodded his yellow head. He was a good friend to have.

How Jimmy worked to teach Lucky! Soon the little dog could run along the tight-rope as fast as Jimmy could. Then Jimmy took his mother into his secret and she made

Lucky a dear little red skirt to wear, and bought her a little parasol to carry over her head—for Lucky could walk on her hind-legs on the tight-rope now. It was marvellous to see her. She loved her tricks and was always anxious to show off.

Jimmy worked at Lucky's other tricks too. She thought nothing of wheeling the doll's pram about and tucking up the doll. She could jump like a hare too, and could hold on to a swing-bar with her teeth and swing like that. She could dance round with Jimmy in time to music, her little hind-legs twinkling in and out merrily. And then Jimmy noticed that she seemed to understand when Sammy did his tricks of counting. When Mr. Wally said to the chimpanzee, "Which is figure 4?" Lucky would go to the right figure even before Sammy picked it himself.

"I believe she could count too—and perhaps spell," thought Jimmy in glee. So he made some big figures and letters and began patiently to teach Lucky.

Lucky learnt easily. Soon she knew all the figures up to five, like Sammy. Then she learnt to spell her own name. This is how Jimmy taught her. He put all the letters of the alphabet out in front of Lucky, and rubbed a piece of meat on to the L. Lucky soon sniffed that out and fetched the letter. Then Jimmy rubbed the meat on the letter U and Lucky fetched *that* out. After that she fetched out C, K, and Y. Jimmy did it all over again—and again—and soon Lucky knew that she had to fetch out the five letters.

"Wuff, wuff!" she said, her little head cocked on to one side. That meant, "I understand, Master. And I understand too that you want special letters fetched out, for some reason or other."

In a week Lucky had learnt to fetch out the five letters of her name, bringing them in the right order—L-U-C-K-Y! When Oona first saw her doing this, he couldn't believe his eyes.

"Now she knows what I want her to do with these letters, it will be easy to teach her other words," said Jimmy, in delight. "And I'm teaching her to do sums, Oona. Listen, Lucky—one bone and two bones—how many?"

Lucky cocked her head one side, her bright eyes shining. She scraped with her paw on the ground three times. Then she barked three times.

"There you are," said Jimmy. "She can do the answer in paw-scrapes or barks—one and two make three!"

"She is a marvellous dog," said Oona. "I will make her a tiny shoe for her right fore-foot, Jimmy, and then when she paws the ground in her answers she will make a knocking sound that everyone will hear. We will stand her on a box."

Lotta knew about Lucky, but she didn't tell anyone. Only when Lucky was quite perfectly trained was Mr. Galliano to know. Then perhaps he would say he would see Lucky and Jimmy at practice in the ring. Jimmy and Lotta watched over Lucky carefully, fed her well, brushed and washed her till her coat shone, and gave her all the love that her little doggy heart needed. She was the happiest dog in the show.

Jimmy would not let Lucky practise her tricks for long at a time, for Lal had told him that little and often was the best way. Any animal got tired and cross if it did the same thing too long. They were like children. But Jimmy did not need to be told of this. He knew without telling everything that was right and good for the animals in his care.

All the same he listened to Lal carefully, for he was always eager to pick up any bits of circus knowledge. He knew all kinds of things now—how to rub resin on to the horses' backs before they went into the ring at night, so that Lotta would not slip when she stood on them—how to test every rope and bolt and pin before Oona or Sticky Stanley the clown did their tricks—how to sense when any animal was not well.

Often one of the grooms would come to Jimmy for help if one of the beautiful stallion horses was restless and nervous. Then Jimmy would speak a few words in the low, gentle voice he always kept for animals, and the horse would listen and calm down. The circus-folk said that Jimmy was as good as Mr. Galliano with the horses— though Mr. Galliano was a marvel with animals, and had been known to go into a cage of angry fighting tigers and calm them at once with a few words.

At last Lucky was perfectly trained. She did all her tricks quickly and smoothly, and even Jimmy could not wish her to do better. Now he would ask Mr. Galliano to see them in the ring.

But what a disappointment for poor Jimmy! Mr. Galliano was in a bad temper that day. Someone whom he had engaged to come to his circus with five beautiful tigers had sent word to say he could not come—and Mr. Galliano roared angrily.

So, when Jimmy went timidly up the steps of the caravan and called Mr. Galliano, he was met by a frowning face and an angry shout.

"Well! What do you want, boy?"

"Please, sir, I've come to ask you if you will see my dog Lucky in the ring with me?" began Jimmy nervously, for, like everyone else, he was frightened of Mr. Galliano when he was angry.

"See you and your dog in the ring!" cried Mr. Galliano. "Indeed I won't! You want to waste my time—yes? Go away—and if you dare to ask me such silly things again I will send you away!"

Of course Mr. Galliano did not mean all this—but Jimmy was very miserable and disappointed as he went

147

back to his own caravan. How he wished he had not asked Mr. Galliano just then—he might have listened if he had not been cross. Poor Jimmy! After he had worked so hard too!

Someone had heard what Mr. Galliano had said—and that someone was Mr. Wally. He remembered how good Jimmy had been when he would not let him help with Sammy in the ring. He ran over to the little boy.

"Cheer up!" he said. "I'll see old Galliano for you tomorrow—and I'll make him see you and Lucky in the ring. You see!"

LUCKY HAS A CHANCE

Jimmy was so pleased when Mr. Wally spoke kindly to him. If only he would see Mr. Galliano and speak for him and Lucky, things might be all right.

"How kind you are, Mr. Wally," he said gratefully.

"Jimmy, I once did you a bad turn," said Mr. Wally, "and instead of paying me back with rudeness and unkindness you were just the same to me as you had always been—helping me with Sammy and doing everything you could. Well, if I can do you a *good* turn now, I will. You couldn't go into the ring any more with Sammy because I wouldn't let you—but I'll get you there with Lucky or my name's not Wally!"

Jimmy could have cried for joy. What his mother said was true then—if you laughed at obstacles and used them as stepping-stones they did really take you somewhere. How much better it would be for Jimmy to go into the ring with his own dog Lucky, than as helper to Mr. Wally with Sammy the chimpanzee!

Mr. Wally kept his word. The next day, when Mr. Galliano had calmed down, and Mrs. Galliano had sent all the circus-folk tins of lobster to make up for Mr. Galliano's bad temper the day before, Mr. Wally asked to have a word with Mr. Galliano.

He disappeared into his caravan with the ring-master. Jimmy waited nearby anxiously.

"Give Jimmy a chance," said Mr. Wally to Mr. Galliano. "I believe he has trained that dog of his till it's almost like a child, Galliano. He's longing to go into the ring again."

"But you kept him out, Wally—yes?" said Mr. Galliano.

"Then why do you speak for the boy now?"

"I speak for him because he is a good boy, one of those few people who pay back good for evil," said Mr. Wally, going red.

Mr. Galliano whistled softly. Mrs. Galliano spoke to him in her slow voice from the back of the caravan.

"You should see him, Galliano. Jimmy is a fine boy."

"Very well, I will see him," said Mr. Galliano. "But it will be a waste of my time, yes. I will see him in the ring with Lucky in an hour's time, Wally."

Jimmy was overjoyed when Mr. Wally came out and told him the news. How glad he was that he had taken his mother's advice and not been horrid to Mr. Wally! If he had he would not have had Mr. Wally's help now. He ran to get Lucky for a little practise on the tight-rope.

In an hour's time Jimmy was in the ring with Lucky. He had dressed himself in his fine circus suit. Lucky had on her quaint little skirt too. She ran about on her hind legs, wuffing in excitement. She knew quite well that something important was going to happen.

"Do your best, Lucky, old girl," said Jimmy. "Do your best!" Lucky licked his ear; and then Mr. Galliano came in — and Mrs. Galliano too. But nobody else was allowed inside the tent.

"Begin," said Galliano — and Jimmy began. He said very little to Lucky — just a word now and again — for Lucky understood a cock of his head, a snap of his fingers, or a whisper better than a shouted command.

First Lucky did the simple things — begging and trusting and jumping and walking on her hind legs carrying a flag, a basket, or a parasol. Then she wheeled the pram and tucked up the doll. Then she walked the tight-rope with Jimmy, running lightly along it on her small feet, with their thin rubber socks on. Mr. Galliano had never seen a dog doing that before and neither had

Mrs. Galliano. They sat and stared as if they were turned to stone — could it be possible that the dog Lucky, who was no more than a puppy, had learnt all these things in a few months?

Then came the counting. Jimmy slipped a little wooden shoe on to Lucky's right fore-foot, and stood her on a wooden stand. He cried out loudly, so that Mr. and Mrs. Galliano might hear. "Lucky, listen to me! If I give you *two* bones and *three* bones, how many will you have?"

Lucky listened, her head on one side. She thought. Then she knocked with her foot — five times.

"Quite right!" cried Jimmy, throwing her a biscuit. "Now listen again. Lucky, if I give you *three* bones and then take away *one*, how many will you have?"

Lucky knocked the answer loudly with her foot — two knocks — then she barked twice as well to show that she really *did* know the answer! Mr. Galliano was astonished.

Then Jimmy brought out the letters of the alphabet and spread them in front of the little dog.

"Bring me the letters of your name, Lucky," he cried—and Lucky found them and brought them to him, one by one—L-U-C-K-Y. Mrs. Galliano clapped. She simply couldn't help it.

And then Jimmy made Lucky do her last trick. "Lucky," he said, "can you tell me the name of the man who owns the best circus on the road?"

Lucky wagged her tail and set off to find the letters she had been taught. And what letters do you think she found? She found 'G-A-L-L-I-A-N-O'. Galliano! Jimmy had had to put two L's and two A's into the alphabet as Galliano's name had two. Wasn't it a long word for a little dog to spell?

Mr. Galliano jumped up from his seat. "Wonderful! Amazing!" he shouted. "This is a dog in a thousand, yes—and she shall go into the ring with you tonight, Jimmy—yes, yes, yes!"

Jimmy went red with joy and thanked Mr. Galliano.

"That dog will make your fortune, yes, without doubt," said the ring-master, and he cracked his whip which he always carried about with him.

Jimmy tore off to tell his mother and Lotta and Lal and Laddo and Oona and Mr. Wally. They were all pleased.

"You must have an even finer circus suit," said Oona. "Yes, you must have one that glitters and sparkles like mine. We will go into the town to an old dressmaker I know, Jimmy, and she will make you a magnificent suit."

"But I haven't much money," said Jimmy.

"You will soon have plenty," laughed Oona. "That dog of yours will earn more in a month than you or I could earn in a year."

Well, from the very beginning of her life in the ring

that night, Lucky was a success. Mr. Galliano had not said anything about Jimmy and Lucky in his circus posters, and so no one knew that they were going to see them that night.

But when the little dog had finished her marvellous tricks, everyone stood up and cheered till they were hoarse! Jimmy had to come into the ring again and again and bow, whilst Lucky ran round and round his legs in delight. People had been astonished enough when Lucky had walked the tight-rope behind Jimmy—but when they saw that the dog could count and spell, they were amazed! Even Sammy the chimp joined in the cheering! Mr. Galliano had never known the people to cheer and clap so madly.

Everyone was pleased at the little boy's success with his dog, for they all liked Jimmy. Oona himself went to fetch Jimmy's new suit when it was done, and squeezed himself into Jimmy's caravan to see the little boy try it on. My goodness! It was like an enchanted suit. It fitted Jimmy tightly from heels to head, and even his toes glittered as he walked, for sequins had been sewn everywhere! He wore a little red velvet cloak over the glittering silver suit, and really, his mother could hardly believe it was Jimmy who stood before her.

There were only a few more days to stay in the place where the circus was then giving its show. Each night Jimmy and Lucky were cheered and clapped, and Mr. Galliano seeing the seats fill up well, and the money pour into the box at the gate, tipped his hat over his right ear so much that it fell right off, and Jemima the monkey ran off with it, much to Lotta's delight.

"I suppose you'll soon be getting too grand to play with me any more, Jimmy," she said one day, as they sat together on the steps of Lotta's caravan, eating buttered buns.

"If you say things like that, Lotta, I shall push you off the steps," said Jimmy. "You ought to know me better — and anyway, it isn't so much *I* that get the claps and cheers — it's Lucky."

"You taught her, though," said Lotta, licking the butter off her bun. "Nobody else could have taught Lucky so well. I heard my mother say so."

"Did she?" said Jimmy, pleased. "Oh, Lotta — I'm so happy! First I wanted to join the circus and never thought it would happen — and it did! Then I wanted to go into the ring, and I did — and then I wanted to take Lucky into the ring, and now that's happened too."

"Yes — you are very lucky," said Lotta. "And I think your dog Lucky will bring you more luck too."

Lotta was right. Lucky brought Jimmy more good fortune. The last night that the circus was giving its show for the town, a big man sat in one of the front seats, watching. When he saw Jimmy come in, all glittering from top to toe, bringing with him his small, dancing dog, the big man sat up. This was what he had really come to see.

He watched carefully, and whistled softly to himself when he saw Lucky counting and spelling. At the end of the show he went to Jimmy's caravan.

Jimmy's mother was there, cooking some bacon and eggs for their supper. The big man spoke to her.

"Are you Jimmy's mother?" he said. "Well, my good woman, I am Mr. Alfred Cyrano, the owner of the biggest circus in the world. I want your boy to leave this circus and come to join mine. I will pay him well. He has a dog there that I could do with in my circus."

At that moment Jimmy came up. Mr. Alfred Cyrano clapped him on the shoulder. "Hey, boy!" he said. "That's a fine dog of yours. I'll buy her from you, and engage you to come to my circus for ten pounds a week. And

I'll give you one hundred pounds for the dog."

Jimmy couldn't say a word. Neither could his mother. One hundred pounds for Lucky—and ten pounds a week to join a bigger circus! It seemed too strange to be true. But then a thought struck Jimmy.

"If you bought Lucky, then she wouldn't be mine," he said. "And suppose you didn't like me after a week or two and sent me away—I would have to leave Lucky behind, wouldn't I?"

"Oh, well, if I buy the dog, she's mine," said Mr. Alfred Cyrano, lighting a cigar about twice as big as Mr. Galliano ever had. Jimmy made up his mind in a flash.

"Then I say no, thank you, sir," he said. "I can't part with Lucky, not even for a *thousand* pounds. She's worth much more than money to me. I love her, and she loves me. And besides, it would be mean to leave Mr. Galliano and all my friends here just as I am beginning to help them to make money. They took me on and were kind to me when I was just a little schoolboy and knew nothing."

"Pah!" said Mr. Alfred Cyrano; "you are a stupid silly boy. One day you will be sorry you did not come with the great Mr. Cyrano!"

He strode off in disgust. When the news got round that Jimmy had said no to Mr. Cyrano, everyone was excited. And then a message came to Jimmy to go to Mr. Galliano's caravan. What *could* he want?

Jimmy did get a surprise when he found out why Mr. Galliano had sent for him!

THE WONDERFUL CARAVAN – AND JUMBO'S SURPRISE

Jimmy set off to Mr. Galliano's caravan. It was late and the little boy was tired. What did Mr. Galliano want with him so late at night?

He went up the steps. Mrs. Galliano opened the caravan door and he went in. It really was a lovely caravan, roomy and comfortable — much, much better than Jimmy's own. Mr. Galliano was sitting at the table eating a plum-pie with cream. He cut Jimmy a big slice, poured cream over it, and pushed it towards the surprised boy.

"Eat," he said. "I want to talk to you, Jimmy. I hear that Mr. Alfred Cyrano came to ask you to sell Lucky to him and go with him to his big circus — yes?"

"Yes, he did, Mr. Galliano," said Jimmy, eating the pie hungrily. "But I said no."

"Why did you say no?" asked Mr. Galliano, and he looked hard at Jimmy.

"Well, Mr. Galliano, sir, there were two reasons," said Jimmy, going red. "I won't sell my dog Lucky to anyone in the world — and I'm not going to leave you, sir, either, when you've given me my first chance."

Mrs. Galliano made a gentle noise rather like the purring of a cat. Mr. Galliano choked over a piece of pie. He swallowed it, cleared his throat, jumped up and gave Jimmy such a clap on the back that the little boy almost fell into his plate of pie.

"He won't leave Galliano — no?" roared Mr. Galliano in delight. "He won't sell his dog — no? He does not want money — no? He loves his dog and his friends before he loves money — yes?"

"Well, Mr. Galliano, I *do* want money really," said Jimmy. "But not if I have to leave you or sell Lucky to get it."

"And what do you want money for, Jimmy?" asked Mrs. Galliano in her soft slow voice, putting a cup of coffee in front of him.

"There's one very special reason I want it for," said Jimmy. "I want my mother to have a fine caravan like this, Mrs. Galliano. She isn't really one of the circus-folk, you see, and she's been used to having plenty of room to move about in. Our caravan is so small and old and ugly, though we've made it look better since we've painted it."

"Now listen to me, Jimmy," said Mr. Galliano, and he sat down and leaned over the table to Jimmy. "You are a loyal and grateful boy, and I tell you those two things are hard to find in anyone. Well—I, too, can be loyal and grateful—yes? Galliano can be a good friend to those who stick to him. You shall have the caravan you want—yes, and all the things in it that you want too! You have said you will stay with me, and I know, Jimmy, that you and your little dog will bring money to the circus. Very well, then—in return I will spend money on you—yes?"

Jimmy's mouth fell open in surprise and delight. Have a caravan like Mr. Galliano's—big, roomy, and beautiful? Whatever would his mother say?

"Oh, Mr. Galliano—thank you!" stammered Jimmy. "I didn't expect anything like that. I do hope I shall be worth it all to you."

"Boys like Jimmy don't grow on every bush, do they, Tessa?" said Mr. Galliano, smiling at his wife. "You shall stay with me till you get too big for my little circus, Jimmy—yes?"

Jimmy said good-night and fell down the steps of the caravan in a great hurry to tell his mother the grand news. What a lucky day it had been for him when he had chosen his puppy Lucky! Lotta had named her well! He bumped into Mr. Tonks as he ran in the dark to his own caravan.

"Now, now, is this a new elephant or an escaped express train?" said Mr. Tonks, sitting down suddenly in the field.

"Whatever's the matter, Jimmy? Are you running a race?"

"No," said Jimmy, and he poured out his story to Mr. Tonks as they sat there in the dewy field.

"Boy, you did well to say no to Mr. Cyrano," said Mr. Tonks solemnly. "He did not want you—he wanted your dog. Two weeks after you had joined his circus he would have sent you off, without Lucky. He is not a good man."

"Well, Mr. Galliano *is*!" said Jimmy. "And I'll never leave him as long as he wants me."

He tore off to his own caravan, where his father and mother were sitting waiting for him, wondering whatever had happened to him.

Jimmy soon told them everything, and they sat up talking till long past midnight. "Oh, if only I can have a really proper caravan, with plenty of room for everything, and a nicely fixed-in stove, I should be really happy," said Mrs. Brown, delighted. Jimmy's father looked proudly at his little boy. Who would have thought he could do so much?

Jimmy didn't sleep much that night. He tossed and turned, and thought of Lucky and Oona and Mr. Tonks and Lotta and Mr. Cyrano and everything. Most of all he thought of the new caravan he was going to get for his mother. Should he go and choose it by himself for a big surprise—or should he take his mother with him and let her choose it? Perhaps it would be best to let her choose it. He fell asleep then, and slept so late that the circus was almost ready to move off on the road again before he awoke. Lotta had fed Lucky and the other dogs. Mrs.

Brown would not let her wake Jimmy.

"We pass a big place that sells caravans on the way to our next show-place," said Mr. Tonks. "It's quite near the place where we shall camp for the night."

"I shall ask Mr. Galliano if I can get it, then!" said Jimmy joyfully. So the next day, with a note from Mr. Galliano in his hand, Jimmy, his mother, and father, all went to the caravan-place. The caravans stood in a great field, ready to be bought. There were all kinds — ones to be hired for two or three weeks — ones to be lived in always, big ones, little ones, blue ones, yellow ones — ones to be pulled by horses and ones to be pulled by cars.

"I say!" said Jimmy, in surprise. "Look at all those caravans, Mother! Whichever shall we choose?"

The man who managed the caravan-place showed them a great many caravans. Mrs. Brown stopped by a yellow one with blue wheels and blue chimney. "Is this very expensive?" she asked. "It is so large and roomy, and everything is fitted so neatly inside. Look, Jimmy, there are even taps to turn on and off, and a place to store water in so that you can get it without always running to the nearest stream! We can fill up whenever we want to, and it will last us for some time."

The man looked at Mr. Galliano's letter. "You could have that one if you wanted to," he said. "It is not any more money than Mr. Galliano says he will pay."

So they chose the yellow caravan. Really, it was wonderful! There was a place for everything. There were bunks to sleep in that folded flat up against the wall to be out of the way in daytime. Mr. Brown said it reminded him of a ship. There were four bunks, but Mrs. Brown said it wouldn't matter, they needn't use the odd one.

There was a fine stove fitted neatly in a corner. There were cupboards all round the sides and under the bench that ran down one side. Underneath the caravan were lockers where all kinds of things could be stored. There was even a folding table, painted yellow!

"I shall hardly need to get anything to go into the caravan!" said Jimmy's mother joyfully. "Just curtains and a clock and a carpet — things like that."

They set off to buy these things. They bought a green carpet and green curtains, and other little things that Mrs. Brown wanted. Really, their caravan would be nicer than anyone else's, except Mr. Galliano's!

"We'll come and fetch the caravan this evening," said Mr. Brown, putting all the things inside it. "We'll bring a horse with us."

But they didn't bring a horse. Mr. Tonks said he would lend them Jumbo, for the horses were tired with their long journey. So, about seven o'clock, Jumbo set off with Jimmy. Mrs. Brown was busy turning the things out of the old caravan and Mr. Brown had plenty of odd jobs to do. Jimmy could quite well fetch the new caravan.

He went along beside Jumbo, who was happy to be with the little boy he loved. They had to pass through a small and busy town on their way to the caravan-field, and a crowd gathered to watch the big elephant pass. Jumbo, was going along quite peacefully when he suddenly stopped, lifted up his trunk and trumpeted long and loudly.

"What's the matter, Jumbo?" said Jimmy, in great surprise. But he was even more surprised when Jumbo left him and lumbered towards the crowd. The people scattered in alarm. Jumbo hurried towards a man who was standing in a doorway. He reached out his trunk and took firm hold of the man.

"Jumbo! Jumbo! What are you doing?" cried Jimmy in a fright. The man struggled, but it was no use, he could not get away from the elephant.

And then suddenly Jimmy saw who the man was. He

was Harry, the bad man who had been odd-job man to the circus before Mr. Brown had joined it—the man who had run off with all the circus money, and had never been found.

A policeman came running up. "What's all this—now what's all this?" he said sternly. "What's your elephant doing?"

"He's caught the man who stole the money from the circus," said Jimmy. "That's Harry in his trunk! Jumbo won't hurt him—he's just got hold of him to take him back to the circus, I expect. Elephants never forget a kindness, or an unkindness, you know—and this man was unkind to Jumbo. Now Jumbo has remembered and has got Harry."

A crowd, with the policeman at the head, followed old Jumbo, who plodded back to the circus, holding Harry firmly. Harry was not in the least hurt, but he was very frightened at the thought of meeting Mr. Galliano, whom he had robbed some months back.

Only when Jumbo was at Mr. Galliano's caravan did he put Harry down—and the policeman at once took hold of his arm. Mr. Galliano appeared in astonishment—and very soon Harry was marched off by the policeman, who had written down in his notebook all about the money Harry had stolen.

"What did I tell you?" said Mr. Tonks to Jimmy and Lotta. "An elephant never forgets! If Harry hadn't teased Jumbo, Jumbo would have passed him by today; but he did him a bad turn, and Jumbo remembered it and caught Harry."

"What an exciting day!" sighed Jimmy, setting off once more with Jumbo to fetch his caravan. He got to the field at last, hitched Jumbo to his lovely yellow caravan and set off back to the camp again. It was dark when he got there, but all the circus-folk were waiting to greet him and cheer the new caravan.

"Hurray! Here comes Jimmy — my, what a fine caravan!" shouted Lotta. How excited all the circus-folk were when they saw the marvellous caravan. They had to look at everything though it was getting very late. But at last the beds were made in three of the four bunks, the door was shut, and the Brown family settled themselves to sleep in their beautiful new home. Lucky had a basket of her own, and she slept proudly on a yellow blanket to match the caravan.

"Good-night, Lucky," said Jimmy sleepily. "You are Lucky by name and lucky by nature! Good-night, best little dog in the world!"

THE TWO MARVELLOUS BROTHERS

When Jimmy awoke the next morning in the new caravan, he looked round in delight. The sun shone through the windows and lighted up everything. All was new and gleaming. How happy his mother would be in a home like this! Jimmy loved living in a house on wheels. It was most exciting.

This circus was moving off to its next show-place early that morning. Soon the Browns were up and took their turn at washing in the fine wash-basin. Jimmy's mother folded back the three bunk-beds out of the way, and set the table for breakfast, which she cooked on the bright little stove in the corner.

"I shall love following the circus and belonging to it now I have a fine new caravan," said Mrs. Brown happily. "I just couldn't bear having to live in a mess and a muddle, and being dirty and untidy, like most of the circus-folk. I like them very much—they are generous and kind-hearted—but, oh dear! they really are not very clean or tidy."

"Perhaps when they see our fine gleaming caravan they will want one like it, and be tidy and clean too," said Jimmy; but Mr. Brown said no, the folk were too old to alter their ways now.

"Lotta's not too old," said Jimmy's mother. "She will see our caravan and perhaps mend her ways a bit, the untidy little thing."

Jimmy laughed. Lotta was certainly untidy, though she could look beautiful enough in the ring, dressed up in her fine clothes. But he did not think that even his mother could make Lotta wash behind her ears each morning.

The circus set off once more. Everyone was talking about how Jumbo had caught Harry the night before, and the elephant was quite a hero. Mr. Tonks was proud of him. Harry would be well punished, there was no doubt of that. Maybe he would not be unkind to an animal again.

On went the circus to its next show-place. There it settled in and once more gave its show every night. Everyone worked hard, and again the circus was a success, especially Jimmy and Lucky. How people stood up and cheered when they saw Lucky following Jimmy on the tight-rope, walking on her hind legs, and carrying her little sunshade! Jimmy and Lucky had their pictures in the papers, and Mrs. Brown cut them out and pinned them on the walls of the caravan.

On went the circus again, and yet again. Always it seemed to be on the move. Sometimes it stayed only three nights at a town, sometimes two or three weeks. Christmas drew near, and Mr. Galliano planned an extra big circus just outside a very big town. He drew up the programme carefully.

"I must get one more turn," he said to Mrs. Galliano. "I will get the two Marvel Brothers, yes. They sit on trapeze seats high in the air, and catch one another as they swing. It is a thing that people love, yes."

So the two Marvel Brothers came to join the circus. They were short, strong men with beautiful straight bodies and bright, clear eyes. They brought with them a thin little dog, a black spaniel with sad brown eyes and floppy ears.

Jimmy made friends with the spaniel that same day. Its name was Lulu, and it snuggled up to Jimmy as if it had known him all its life.

"Lotta, isn't this dog thin?" said Jimmy, feeling it. "I wonder if there's anything wrong with it."

"Perhaps the Marvel Brothers don't feed it enough," said Lotta. "I'll give her some biscuits when I next feed our own dogs. I don't much like those two new circusmen, Jimmy. They smile too much."

"Smile too much?" said Jimmy, in surprise. "What do you mean?"

"Well, you watch them next time you see them," said Lotta. "They smile with their mouths and show all their lovely white teeth — but they don't smile with their eyes like you do and everyone else."

Lotta was right. Jan and Yol, the two trapeze performers, never smiled with their eyes — but they smiled with their mouths a hundred times a day, saying wonderful things to everyone, and trying to make people think they were the most marvellous brothers in the world.

They certainly *were* marvellous. The first time Jimmy saw them swinging on their bar-swings, high up in the top of the big tent, flying from one swing to another, and catching one another in mid-air, he gazed in astonishment. He was dreadfully afraid they would fall.

"Fall!" said Jan scornfully, when Jimmy told him this one day. "You do not know what you are talking about, boy. I have been doing these things since I was two. My father and my mother, my grandfather and my great-grandfather, were all trapeze-folk."

The spaniel, Lulu, came up just then and sprawled over Jan's feet. He kicked it away impatiently. Jimmy went red with anger.

"Don't do that," he said. "You hurt the dog."

"Well, it's my dog, isn't it?" said Jan, and he would have kicked the spaniel again if it had not gone out of his reach. Jimmy didn't say a word more. He went off to tell Lotta. She nodded her head.

"They are clever men, but not good," she said. "Don't let Lucky go near them, Jimmy."

Jimmy was careful to keep Lucky away from the Marvel Brothers, for after he had told Jan not to kick Lulu, both brothers seemed to dislike him.

Then another thing happened that made Jimmy even more careful. His father had to put up and test the big steel posts and bars from which the strong swings hung on which Jan and Yol swung each night. Mr. Brown was always careful to see that these were exactly right, for he knew that if anything went wrong, Jan or Yol might fall.

One night Jan missed catching his brother as Yol came flying through the air from his swing. Yol fell into the net below, where he bounced up and down. He was soon up again and on his swing—but Mr. Galliano was angry.

"If you do that again I shall not pay you so much money," he told the two sulky brothers. "You know why you made that mistake? It is because you do not practise enough. You will practise every day from now—yes?"

"It wasn't our fault," said Jan; "the posts were not put up right. They had slipped a little. Brown had not done the job well."

So Jimmy's father was called to Mr. Galliano's caravan. But he knew quite well that he had tested every screw, every post, every bar—and Mr. Galliano believed him, for he had found Brownie to be an honest and truthful man.

This made Jan and Yol dislike Jimmy even more, and they lay in wait for him behind caravans and tripped him up. The little boy was not used to people disliking him and it made him very unhappy. Also he was dreadfully afraid they might harm Lucky. He took her with him wherever he went.

Lulu the spaniel tried to go with Jimmy as much as she could. Jimmy fed her, for he knew quite well she didn't get enough food from Jan and Yol. Lulu lay on the steps of Jimmy's caravan all day long. She loved Jimmy and

Lotta. But Jan and Yol were angry when they found that their dog followed the boy and girl about so much. They whipped her and shut her up in their own caravan, where she howled and scratched at the door for hours.

Jimmy and Lotta dared not let Lulu out, but they were miserable about it. The brothers' caravan was right at the end of the circus-field, and nobody but the two children could hear the dog. They didn't know what to do.

"I wish they'd never come to the circus," said Jimmy gloomily. "They are the first people I haven't liked."

"Oh, all circus-people aren't nice," said Lotta, laughing at Jimmy's gloomy face. "But it's funny to meet two that don't like animals. Most circus-folk love them."

"They've been telling everyone that my father doesn't do his work properly," said Jimmy. "I don't mind what they say about *me*—but I won't have them saying things about my father."

"Brownie is a good sort," said Lotta, who was very fond of Jimmy's father. "Cheer up, Jimmy. Let's go and take the dogs for a walk."

"I wish we could take Lulu too," said Jimmy. But that was impossible.

That night, when the Marvel Brothers went up the steps of their caravan and opened the door, they fell headlong over Lulu, who rushed to welcome them. Yol hit his head against a chair and fell into a great rage.

He picked up a whip and beat poor Lulu hard. Then he turned the dog out into the bitter frosty night and banged the door on her. The little dog lay under the caravan, shivering with cold. After a while she crept to Lotta's caravan, which was the nearest, and whined. Lotta, who always awoke at a dog's bark or whine, sat up and listened. Lulu whined again.

In a trice the little girl was out of bed and lit a candle.

She opened the door and saw poor Lulu there, bleeding from a cut over her eye where Yol had hit her very hard. Lotta threw on a coat, slipped out of the caravan, and went to wake Jimmy. The two children bathed the dog's cut, whispered angrily about Yol and Jan, and then Jimmy put Lucky at the foot of his own bed, and put Lulu into Lucky's basket. She was still shivering with cold, so he heated some milk for her and covered her up well.

In the morning Lotta and Jimmy went to Mr. Galliano with Lulu. They told him how she had come to them in the middle of the night, cold and hurt. Mr. Galliano listened and his face grew dark.

"No one shall stay in my circus who is cruel to an animal," he said. "Hey, Mr. Wally! Tell Jan and Yol I want to see them."

Jan and Yol came, smiling and showing their strong white teeth. Jimmy and Lotta had gone with Lulu. Mr. Galliano was standing by his caravan, whip in hand, his top-hat perfectly straight on his head.

"Here is your money," he said to the two surprised brothers. "Take it and leave. I will not have anyone with me who treats a dog as you treat yours. You will leave the dog behind, yes."

"But, Mr. Galliano," said Jan, forgetting to smile, "you can't do this. We bring hundreds of people to see your Christmas circus. We are famous."

"I don't care if nobody comes at all," said Mr. Galliano, with a loud crack of his whip. "You are clever, yes, but it is not enough to be clever only. Leave this morning."

The two brothers did not dare to say any more. With dark, sulky faces they rolled away in their green caravan, leaving Lulu behind. Jimmy and Lotta watched them go. Everyone was glad.

"Good old Galliano!" said Lilliput, who was wearing Jemima the monkey round his neck as usual. "Trust him

169

to send off any rascals, even if he loses money in doing so."

"He made them leave Lulu behind, and they did," said Jimmy. "Lotta and I are going to share her. She isn't at all clever, but she is a loving, gentle creature, and Lucky loves her."

"Jan and Yol would not dare to take Lulu with them after Galliano had forbidden them to," said Lilliput. "He could send word to every circus in the country, and no one would take the Marvel Brothers again. I have heard that they have been turned out of two other circuses before this."

"Woof!" said Lulu, and tugged at Jimmy's bootlace. "I am glad to be your dog now. Woof!"

LOTTA IS UNHAPPY

The Christmas holidays were over, and the month of January was slipping away. The circus had done well all through Christmas and afterwards, and now it was on the move again. It had a long way to go to its next show-place, and Jimmy was pleased to think that his mother had such a big, comfortable caravan to live in. He was very proud of the spick-and-span home on wheels that he had been able to get for her.

Jimmy's mother kept it beautifully, too—not as most of the caravans were kept. The circus-folk were kindly, generous, brave people, but they were not very clean and dreadfully untidy. Lotta was beginning to be much cleaner and tidier, though—she was brushing her pretty hair every day and tying it back, and her face at least was clean. She was better at her lessons too, and was reading very well.

Lal was delighted. She came to see Mrs. Brown one day and thanked her.

"Lotta is a different child since you and Jimmy came," she said, pleased. "She was such a little harum-scarum thing, and I wasn't much good at dealing with her—but now I am quite proud of her."

"Well, you've done a lot for Jimmy too," said Mrs. Brown. "You and Laddo have taught him to ride well, and helped him with animals—and you bought him his wonderful dog, Lucky."

Jimmy and Lotta were always together. They sometimes quarrelled, especially when Lotta had one of her naughty days, when she made faces and pinched and punched poor Jimmy all for nothing—but they always made it up, and thought the world of one another.

"Won't it be lovely when the spring days come and we can go for walks in the early morning?" said Lotta, who loved the fresh dawns of the countryside. "We shall be at Westsea for Easter, and that's a lovely place—we can take the dogs out for a run on the beach before breakfast each day."

"I shall love the summer again too," said Jimmy. "The smell of the May as we go down the lanes—and the birds singing—and the blue sky, like forget-me-nots—lovely!"

They were sitting in Jimmy's caravan, whilst Mrs. Brown did some mending. It was too cold to sit on the caravan steps now when the circus was moving. The cold wind came and nipped their legs and hands and made them shiver there. Mrs. Brown would not let them get cold—so they had to come inside, and talk and play there.

It was fun to look out of the big side-window and see the towns they passed. Jimmy felt quite sorry for people who lived in houses now. A home on wheels was such fun—you could go where you liked, see fresh places and new people, and then, when the time came, off you went again on rumbling wheels! Lovely!

After a whole week's travelling the circus came to its next show-place. It was February now, and the days were beginning to get longer. The birds sang madly in the early morning. Jimmy lay and listened to them. He tried to whistle as they did, and sometimes his imitation was so good that the blackbirds answered him, and the starlings sat on the chimney of the caravan and made fizzy, spluttery noises, thinking there was another starling down below.

The little boy was very happy and so was Lotta—until a dreadful thing happened.

Jimmy had noticed Lal and Laddo, Lotta's father and mother, looking rather grave and solemn the last few days, but neither he nor Lotta knew why. Sometimes they had sent Lotta out of the caravan, saying they wanted to talk over something. It was all most mysterious.

Jimmy wondered what it was all about—and then he knew. One morning he missed Lotta and couldn't find her anywhere. He hunted all round the circus-field. He asked Oona and Lilliput and Mr. Tonks if they had seen the little girl, but nobody had. She really seemed to have quite disappeared.

"Wherever can she be?" thought Jimmy, quite worried. And then at last he found her.

She was huddled underneath her own caravan, curled up in a big old box that stood on its side. And she was crying bitterly, with Lulu the spaniel licking her face.

Jimmy crawled under the caravan, alarmed. It was so unlike Lotta to cry. Whatever could be the matter?

"Lotta! What is it? Come out and tell me!" he begged.

But Lotta wouldn't come out, and she wouldn't stop crying. Her face was dirty and tear-stained and her eyes were swollen. Jimmy sat down beside her and put his arm round her. The little girl snuggled against him and cried hot tears all down his shirt.

"Lotta, you might tell me what's the matter," said Jimmy. "Are you ill? Have you been punished for something?"

Lotta did not answer at first—but gradually her sobs stopped and she began to speak.

"Oh, Jimmy! Lal and Laddo are leaving the circus—and they're not taking me with them. And I've got to go to Uncle Benjy and live with him—till they come back."

Jimmy's heart sank. It was bad enough that Lal and Laddo were leaving, but Lotta too—that was dreadful!

"I shall be so lonely and miserable," said Lotta, her tears dripping down Jimmy's shirt again. "I like Uncle B-b-b-benjy—but I can't bear to live in a house—I want to be with the circus—and you."

"Why aren't Lal and Laddo taking you with them?" asked Jimmy, surprised, for Lal and Laddo were fond of their clever little girl.

"Because they are going to Hungary for six months, to join Lal's brother there," said Lotta. "He is running a circus at Budapest, Lal says—and will pay them well if they go. And they want to buy new horses out there too. But they are not allowed to take *me*."

She began to cry again, and Jimmy hugged her hard. Poor, poor Lotta! She belonged to the circus. She had never lived in a house. She would be so miserable with Uncle Benjy—she would have to go to school there, and she wouldn't understand that a bit. She would miss her horses and Lal and Laddo—and Jimmy—dreadfully.

"When are they going?" asked Jimmy.

"After this show is finished," said Lotta, rubbing her dirty little hand over her wet face. "They have told Mr. Galliano already. He is getting somebody else instead for Easter. They will bring their own horses, because Lal and Laddo are taking theirs with them."

Jimmy was worried. That meant Lotta would go away very soon—in a few weeks. Whatever would he do without her? The little boy did not know what to say to comfort Lotta. As he sat curled up under the caravan with her, he heard Mr. Galliano shouting:

"Jimmy! Jimmy! Where are you?"

"Here, Mr. Galliano!" cried Jimmy, and he scrambled out. He ran to Mr. Galliano, and saw, to his surprise, that the ring-master's top-hat was on perfectly straight. What could have happened to make him put it on like that?

"Jimmy, go to your mother," said Mr. Galliano. "She has fallen over something and has hurt her leg. Your father has gone for the doctor."

Jimmy went pale. He loved his mother best in all the world. He sped off to the caravan, forgetting all about poor Lotta.

Mrs. Brown was lying on her bed, looking ill. She smiled at Jimmy as he came up the steps.

"Don't worry, dear," she said. "I've only twisted my ankle. It will soon be better."

"What a dreadful morning this is!" thought Jimmy, putting some milk in a saucepan to heat for his mother. "First poor Lotta—and now Mother!"

The doctor soon came. He looked at Mrs. Brown's leg. She had twisted it badly, and the ankle was very swollen.

"Nothing very terrible," said the doctor cheerily, "but you'll have to lie up for two or three weeks, Mrs. Brown."

"Oh dear, I can't do that," said Mrs. Brown, alarmed. "Why, who would look after Jimmy and my husband? Who would cook their meals and see to the caravan?

No — I couldn't do that. I can't stay in bed!"

"You'll have to," said the doctor, looking grave. "If you don't, that foot of yours will give you great trouble."

"I'll see that Mother rests her foot, Doctor," said Jimmy. "I can do everything for her."

"No, Jimmy, you can't," said Mrs. Brown. "You and Daddy are busy all day long — you won't have time to spare to do my work too. I shall get up tomorrow."

The doctor said no more. He went down the steps, and Jimmy and Mr. Brown thanked him for coming and paid him. Lotta was standing a little way off, her face still tear-stained.

"Jimmy," she said, running up, "what's the matter with your mother? Is she badly hurt?"

"No," said Jimmy. "It's just her foot. She's got to rest it for two or three weeks — and she's worried because she won't be able to cook for us and look after the caravan. What a horrid day this is, Lotta."

Lotta looked at Jimmy's sad face and forgot her own troubles. "Jimmy, don't forget what you once told me your mother said, when troubles come," she said. 'Tread on them and they will be stepping-stones to lead you to something good.' Don't worry — I'll come and help each day."

"I don't see what good can possibly come out of a thing like this," said Jimmy gloomily. "Or out of your troubles either, Lotta."

"Don't look like that, Jimmy," said Lotta, who was trying to be brave. "I'll promise to be good over my disappointment if you'll promise not to worry too much about your mother, and will let me help all I can."

"You're a good friend, Lotta," said Jimmy. "All right — we'll both be brave. I don't see how anything nice can possibly come out of this — how can we use troubles like these as stepping-stones to something better? Oh, how horrid everything is! But I must try not to worry."

Lotta ran up the caravan steps to tell Mrs. Brown she would come and help each day. Mrs. Brown was glad. She loved the little girl — and Lotta knew by now just how Mrs. Brown liked things done. She knew that Mrs. Brown liked her stove kept clean. She knew that she liked the floor washed every day. She knew just how Mrs. Brown did her cooking. Oh, Lotta, knew a great deal, nowadays, that she hadn't known before.

Jimmy went off to see to the dogs, and left Lotta to help his mother into bed. Lucky came to him, dancing about merrily, trying to make her little master smile. But Jimmy had no smiles that day. He could not forget that he was soon to lose his best friend — dear, naughty little Lotta.

Lotta began to forget her own troubles in helping Mrs. Brown. She got her comfortably to bed and saw to her poor foot. She ran out to get something for dinner. She put it on to cook, and chattered away to Mrs. Brown. She laid the tiny table beautifully, and Mrs. Brown thought what a clever, handy little girl she was.

Lotta and Jimmy were plucky that day. They did not tell Mrs. Brown a word about Lal and Lotta leaving. They kept their unhappiness to themselves, and smiled and talked to Mrs. Brown at dinner-time to keep her happy and cheerful. She was so pleased.

"I don't know what I should do without, you, Lotta!" she said.

JIMMY AND LOTTA GET THEIR REWARD

The days passed by. Mrs. Brown's foot was slow in getting better, and she was still not able to walk; but she did not mind now, for Lotta spent every minute she could with her, cleaning up the caravan, washing, cooking the meals, and talking to Mrs. Brown in her cheerful voice.

Jimmy was proud of Lotta, for he knew how sad the little girl's heart was, as the days went by, and the time came nearer when she must leave the circus and go to live with Uncle Benjy, so far away. He wished Lotta could write better—for he was afraid she would never be able to write a proper letter to him. Six months seemed years and years—and perhaps Lal and Laddo might not come back even then.

One day three new people came to see Mr. Galliano. They were the riders that Mr. Galliano was going to have instead of Lal and Laddo. There were two women and one man, big strong folk, with kindly faces and ready smiles. Jimmy liked them at once. Their horses had come in a great box-like caravan, and Jimmy went to look at them. They were magnificent animals sleek, silky and good-tempered.

The three new riders—their names were Juanita, Pepita, and Lou—came over to their horses when they had finished talking to Mr. Galliano. They looked at the little boy and smiled. Juanita pointed to Lucky, who was dancing round her.

"This is the famous dog, Lucky?" she asked, in a soft, husky voice. "And you are Jimmy? We have heard of you."

Jimmy went red with pride. To think that he was getting famous already! He didn't know what to say. Sticky

Stanley the clown, who was nearby, grinned and said:

"Oh, our Jimmy will have a circus of his own one day—won't you, Jimmy? He'll be the famous Mr. Jimmiano, and wear a top-hat twice as big as Mr. Galliano's."

Jimmy laughed. He patted the nearest horse. "These *are* lovely horses," he said. "If you want any help with them, let me know. I always helped with Lal's and Laddo's horses each day, and so did Lotta."

"Then you shall help with ours," said Lou, and he smiled at the little boy. "And Lotta too, whoever she is."

"She's a wonderful rider," said Jimmy shyly. "You should just see the things she can do on horseback."

Jimmy was pleased that the three new circus-folk were nice—but how he wished that Lal and Laddo were not going! But they were—their horses and dogs were already being packed into their travelling stables. It would not be long now before they went, and then Lotta would be put into the train and sent off to Uncle Benjy.

Mrs. Brown had heard that Lal and Laddo were going, but she thought that Lotta was going with them. She was sorry to think that Jimmy would lose his little friend, but as he said nothing to her, she thought perhaps he did not mind very much after all.

"I shall miss you very much, Lotta," she said to the little girl. "You have been very good to me these two or three weeks. I wish you were not going away with Lal and Laddo."

"I'm not going with them," said Lotta, her eyes filling with tears. "They can't take me. I've got to go and live with my Uncle Benjy—in a house—and I shall hate it."

Mrs. Brown stared in surprise. "Don't cry, dear," she said. "Come here and tell me all about it. You and Jimmy didn't say anything about this to me."

"I know," sobbed Lotta; "we didn't want you to worry about us when you had a bad foot, and we thought that if we were brave, perhaps something good would come out of these horrid things—but nothing has. And I'm going on Saturday."

Mrs. Brown patted the unhappy little girl, and thought hard. "Brave, kind children," she thought. "Here's Lotta being so kind and good to me all these days when she was unhappy, and Jimmy not saying a word."

Then an idea came into her head. There was a fourth bunk-bed in the caravan—could she possibly keep Lotta with her and Jimmy, till Lal and Laddo came back? Lotta was a dear, useful child, and Mrs. Brown loved her. She could not bear to think of her going away all by herself to her Uncle Benjy—living in a house for the first time in her life—going to school and being laughed at because she did not know her lessons very well. Mrs. Brown hugged the little girl.

"Ask your mother and father if they can spare a minute to speak to me," she said to Lotta. The little girl dried her eyes and ran off. Soon Lal and Laddo came up the steps to see Mrs. Brown.

"Run off and talk to Jimmy for a few minutes," Mrs. Brown said to Lotta. The little girl went away. Mrs. Brown smiled at Lal and Laddo.

"I only heard a few minutes ago that you were not taking Lotta with you," she said. "Now I love the child very much, and she is fond of us all. Don't send her away to her uncle's. Let *me* keep her for you till you come back. She will be happy here in our caravan with Jimmy and Brownie and me."

Lal's face beamed. "Oh, Mrs. Brown! Would you really take our Lotta for us? We hate to send her away, but she cannot stay in the circus alone. She would be so happy with you, and you would look after her well."

"She would be a daughter to you," said Laddo. "She will do more for you than she will for us."

180

"Well, that's settled then," said Mrs. Brown, pleased. "Now perhaps you'll find Jimmy and Lotta and send them here, and I will tell them. They both deserve a bit of good luck."

The two children came up the steps, wondering why they had been sent for. Mrs. Brown smiled at them.

"I just want to tell you that something good has come out of our troubles," she said. "Lotta is to stay with us, Jimmy — she is not to go to her uncle's. She is to live in our caravan, and have the empty bed!"

The two children stared as if they could not believe their ears. Then they went quite mad with delight. They hugged Mrs. Brown. They hugged one another. They danced round the caravan and knocked over two saucepans, a stool, and candlestick. They jumped on the bed and off again. Really, Mrs. Brown couldn't help laughing at the two of them.

Lotta suddenly burst into tears, but she was laughing all the time she was crying. "I'm not really c-c-c-crying," she wept; "it's only because I do feel so g-g-g-glad."

"Well, it's a funny way of showing it," said Mrs. Brown. "You deserve a nice surprise, both of you — you've been brave, good children, and I haven't heard a grumble from either of you."

"Mrs. Galliano says grumblers get all the bad luck going," grinned Jimmy. "So you won't catch *me* grumbling, Mother. Oh, I say, Lotta — you'll be able to ride the horses that Juanita, Pepita, and Lou have brought with them — and maybe if you're good and patient they'll let you go in the ring with them."

"Oh, let me go into the ring with *you* and Lucky!" begged Lotta, bouncing on the bed again. "We could make up a fine turn together."

"What fun we'll have these six months!" cried Jimmy, doing a noisy dance on the floor of the caravan. "Oh,

I was so down in the dumps—and now I'm up in the sky!"

"Well, you don't sound like it," said Mrs. Brown, as Jimmy danced noisily about. "I'm sure clouds wouldn't be so noisy. Stop now, Jimmy, and go with Lotta to buy something for a nice meal."

The children jumped down to the ground, as happy as blackbirds in spring. Jimmy ran to his special secret box where he kept his money. He took out a lot and Lotta's eyes opened wide. "I didn't know you were so rich, Jimmy," she said. "What are you taking all that for?"

"Wait and see!" said Jimmy, making a face at Lotta. She made one back and they laughed. They were too happy for anything.

They went to the town and bought a fine meal, and then Jimmy went to a big draper's shop—and what do you suppose he bought? He asked to see blankets and sheets and a mattress and eiderdown!

"They are for your little bunk-bed," said Jimmy. "My present to you, Lotta! You shall be warm and cosy at night in our caravan."

Lotta was excited. She had never had such lovely bedclothes before. In fact, she had never even slept between sheets before. Most of the circus-folk had rugs or blankets, but very seldom sheets. How grand Lotta would be!

Mrs. Brown laughed when she saw the two children coming home so laden. Lucky carried the basket of food in her mouth—she was a great help at shopping. They all crowded into the cosy caravan and then unpacked everything for Mrs. Brown to see.

Mr. Brown came in then, and had to be told the great news. He was delighted, for he too loved Lotta, and had been very pleased with the way the little girl had looked after them all whilst Mrs. Brown had had a bad foot.

"We shall be a jolly family of four now," he said,

smiling at them all as he sat down to his meal.

"No, five, Dad!" said Jimmy, as Lucky jumped up on his knee. "Don't forget Lucky! You've been a great big piece of luck, haven't you, little dog?"

"Wuff!" said Lucky, neatly taking half a sausage off Jimmy's plate.

It was a very happy meal. Lotta looked round the bright, airy caravan and was glad to think it was to be her home for many months. She was glad to know she was not to leave the circus and, best of all, was not to leave Jimmy. They all began to talk excitedly.

"I'm going to help Jimmy with Lucky!"

"And Lotta's going to ask if she can go in the ring with the three new riders," said Jimmy. "They are such nice folk—I'm sure they will let Lotta do her turn."

"And my foot is much better today, so I shall be able to get about and look after my large family," said Mrs. Brown.

"And I shall keep you all in order and see that you don't get too famous," laughed Mr. Brown.

"Wuff, wuff, wuff!" said Lucky, joining in.

Well, Lal and Laddo went off with their horses and dogs, glad to think that their little Lotta was left behind in the care of such kind people. The circus packed up again, for it had to go on the road to its Easter show-place, where a splendid performance was to be given. A great bustle and hurry was in the camp, and Mr. Galliano cracked his whip and shouted orders for hours on end. Lotta and Jimmy loved it all. It was exciting.

And now, see, the circus is moving off once more! Here come the very fine row of black horses, with one of the grooms, dressed in red, sitting on the front horse, blowing a horn! How grand he looks!

Then comes a carriage that looks as if it is made of gold—and who is this handsome plump man and this smiling black-haired woman by his side? Why, the famous Mr. Galliano and his wife, of course! See him take off his hat and bow to all the watching people and children as if he were a king! See his fine moustache with sharp-pointed ends that turn upwards, and his shiny black top-hat!

Now the white horses come, and with them are Juanita, Pepita, and Lou, for these are the horses they brought with them. Pepita rides the first one proudly, looking as pretty as a picture in a blue, shiny frock. Behind comes Sticky Stanley the clown, dressed in red and black, with his high-pointed hat, turning cart-wheel somersaults all the way, much to the delight of the watching children.

And then a long string of gaily-coloured caravans — a red one — a blue one — a green one — and last of all a beautiful yellow one with pretty curtains flying in the breeze. On the steps, cuddling a black spaniel, sit a pair of children — Jimmy and Lotta, for it is their caravan. How all the children stare at the circus boy and girl and wish they belonged too!

And here comes the elephant, good old Jumbo, patient and kindly as ever, pulling three heavy cages behind him. Mr. Tonks walks by his side, and sometimes Jumbo puts his trunk round his trainer's neck as if it were an arm. That makes everyone laugh.

Here are two open cages — one with Sammy, the chimpanzee, inside, eating a banana and throwing the peel at anyone he sees. Mr. Wally is sitting with him. In the next cage are three monkeys, sitting in a row on a perch, dressed in warm red coats; and riding on the step of their cage is a little man — Lilliput, of course — with his beloved monkey, Jemima, round his neck as usual. Ah, we know all the circus-folk well now!

But who is this marching along on hind legs carrying a flag, as proud as a general? Why, it is Lucky, little dog Lucky, who knows quite well that she will get biscuits if she shows off like this. Yes — too many biscuits.

Jimmy whistles to her. Lucky drops down on her four feet and races off, her flag in her mouth. Good old Lucky! You love your little master best in the world, don't you?

"Good-bye, good-bye!" the watching children call. "Come back soon! Good-bye, Galliano's circus!"

And we too must say good-bye; but if you hear of Mr. Galliano's circus coming to *your* town, go and see how Jimmy and Lotta and Lucky are getting on.

Good luck, Mr. Galliano!

lots. He worked off damages to the farmer whose stock he had decimated. Then he moved to the next town and graduated to horses. Cut the throats of half a herd before he was apprehended.'

'A juvenile psychopath with a blood lust.'

'People simply wrote him off as the village idiot in those days,' said McComb. 'Psychotic motivation was not in their dictionaries. They failed to understand that a boy who slaughtered animals for the hell of it was only one step away from doing the same to humans. Roubaix was sentenced to two years in jail for the horse bloodbath, but because of his age, fourteen, he was allowed to live with the constable, working off his time as a gardener and houseboy. Not long after his release, people in the surrounding countryside began to find the bodies of tramps and drunks who had been strangled.'

'Where did all this take place?'

'A radius of fifty miles around the present city of Moose Jaw, Alberta.'

'Surely Roubaix was arrested as a prime suspect?'

'The Mounties didn't work as fast in the nineteenth century as we do now,' McComb admitted. 'By the time Roubaix was tied to the crimes, he had fled into the virgin forests of the Northwest Territory and didn't turn up again until Riel's rebellion in eighteen eighty-five.'

'The revolt by the descendants of French traders and Indians,' said Villon, recalling his history.

'Métis, they were called. Louis Riel was their leader. Roubaix joined Riel's forces and enshrined himself in Canadian legend as our most prolific killer.'

'What about the time he was missing?'

'Six years,' McComb replied. 'Nothing recorded. There was a rash of unsolved killings attributed to him, but no solid evidence or eyewitness accounts. Only a pattern that hinted of the Roubaix touch.'

'A pattern?'

'Yes, all the victims were done in by injuries inflicted on the throat,' said McComb. 'Mostly from strangulation. Roubaix had turned away from the messy use of a knife. No great fuss was made at the time. People had a different set of moral codes then. They looked upon a scourge who eliminated undesirables as a community benefactor.'

'I seem to remember he became a legend by killing a number of Mounties during Riel's rebellion.'

'Thirteen, to be exact.'

'Roubaix must have been a very strong man.'

'Not really,' replied McComb. 'Actually he was described as frail of build and rather sickly. A doctor who attended him before his execution testified that Roubaix was racked by consumption – what we now call tuberculosis.'

'How was it possible for such a weakling to overpower men who were trained for physical combat?' asked Villon.

'Roubaix used a garrotte made from rawhide not much thicker than a wire. A nasty weapon that cut half-way into his victim's throat. Caught them unaware, usually when they were asleep. Your reputation is well known in body-building circles, Mr Villon, but I daresay your own wife could choke you away if she slipped Roubaix's garrotte around your neck some night in bed.'

'You talk as if the garrotte still exists.'

'It does,' said McComb. We have it on display in the criminal section of the Mountie museum, if you care to view it. Like some other mass killers who cherished a favourite murder weapon, Roubaix lavished loving care on his garrotte. The wooden hand grips that attach to the thong are intricately carved in the shape of timber wolves. It's really quite a piece of craftsmanship.'

'Perhaps I'll have a look at it when my schedule permits,' said Villon without enthusiasm. He pondered a moment, trying to make sense out of Sarveux's instructions to Danielle in the hospital. It didn't add up. A riddle of ciphers. Villon took a flyer on another tack. 'If you had to describe Roubaix's case, how would you sum it up in a single sentence?'

'I'm not sure I know what you're after,' said McComb.

'Let me put it another way. What was Max Roubaix?'

There was silence for a few moments. Villon could almost hear the gears turn in McComb's head. Finally the Mountie said, 'I guess you could call him a homicidal maniac with a fetish for the stranglehold.'

Villon tensed and then relaxed again. 'Thank you,